It Was a Magical Place

Pat Dewees

Table Six Books

ISBN: 979-8-9900198-0-5 (paperback)
ISBN: 979-8-9900198-1-2 (e-book)

This book is a work of autobiographical fiction. Although based on the author's memories, the events in this story did not necessarily happen at the same time or in the same manner they are described in this story or may not have happened at all. The names of the characters based on the author's memories have been changed. Other characters are purely products of the author's imagination. The names and locations of places that inspired this story have been changed.

Cover design by David Provolo

patdeweesauthor.com

Dedicated to my special circle of friends
who were there for me as I worked
to get this book out there.
If you are one of them,
you know I am talking about you.

Chapter One

2024

The bus was late. It is often a little bit late but this time it was very late. It came though and I climbed aboard. The scenery on the commute home from work was always the same. Soon I would be out of the Portland city limits and later I would be in my suburban home in Hillsboro. Early on the bus moved at a normal speed. Soon after my ride began however it slowed to almost a snail's pace. It was because traffic was this slow. The nice thing about riding the bus is it eliminates the stress of driving myself. If the vehicle was in an accident, I would at least always have the comfort of knowing it was not my fault. But buses are subject to slow traffic too.

I suspected there was a snag somewhere in the traffic. I wondered what and where it was. After what seemed like an eternity, I saw the problem. It wasn't a car accident as it usually is. This time it was something different. First, I noticed smoke on the highway ahead of us as I looked out the window. Later I saw the source of the smoke, a brush fire in the highway median. Forest fires are bad this year, even worse than they usually are at this time of the year. Firefighters from a fire truck on the other side of the highways extinguished the median fire. Cars (and buses such as this one) were having to merge into one lane at a point where a fire truck was in the other lanes. There was some comfort in knowing the source of the problem but knowing did not solve the problem. The bus I was on had to work through the traffic.

After another eternity the bus was clear of the fire engine. The transit bus was now moving at normal speed, but it would still be some time until I got home. On the way, I thought about the stories I had seen on the news about people who lost their homes to forest fires. Although the people living in the house usually got out safe, I felt deep sadness for them. They were probably losing cherished links to past memories such as photo albums, wedding albums, collected comic books, and the like. Old fashioned analog photographs stored in old fashioned photo albums could be preserved by scanning them or taking pictures of these pictures with a digital camera, but the process was time consuming and probably not undertaken by many people. Families could take these items with them along with their essentials, but they would have to have both the time to get them as well as space in their vehicles to take them. Many families probably did not have both.

When the bus arrived at my stop, I hopped off and walked one or two thousand feet to my house. I opened the door, disabled the security system, and turned on the television. I was anxious to see if the local news was talking about the brush fire I saw. They were talking about a fire, but it was a much bigger fire that was being televised on the local news. Not only were they talking about it, but the fire also seemed to dominate the news. They were even covering it during the minutes when the weather and sports were usually covered. It was a forest fire on the other side of the Columbia River in the state of Washington. It seemed like there had been a lot of forest fires. People in Oregon and the adjacent state of Washington take great care in preserving our natural world. This is something in which I take great pride. It seems however like that is not enough. One forest fire I had heard about a little more than a month ago burned an area the size of Connecticut not far from here.

That however was not what troubled me the most. What the TV reporter's voice in the background reported here is what was hardest on me.

"Right now, the wildfire is threatening Camp Sunbeam. The camp which happens to be in session is being evacuated as a precaution."

It made me feel a little bit better that the reporter was saying it was just a precaution, but I did not want there to be any chance that the camp was destroyed or even damaged. For me there was much more at stake than rustic buildings. There was even more at stake to me than the trees on the camp property. Memories of one week I spent one summer at that camp began flooding back to me.

Chapter Two

Saturday, June 29, 1985

I t was a magical place. It was the kind of place where anything could happen. It didn't matter that I didn't have a driver's license. Everything was just a short walk away. For that week when I was away from my family, a group of boys slightly younger than me and two boys slightly older than all of us, all residing in the same cabin, *was* my family. There was something about the air at camp that made me feel stronger and more adventurous. That was always the first thing I noticed when I stepped out of my mother's car each of the years I went to camp. This was my third consecutive year to go to camp in the summer. I was sixteen years old. The age range for campers at Camp Sunbeam is eight to fifteen. I was above the age limit but Benjamin Heimer, the director, was a good friend of my mother's and he let me come anyway.

This was my first time at a coed camp session. The first two years, I went to boys' camp. Now Camp Sunbeam only offered girls' camp and coed camp. There just were not enough boys going to Camp Sunbeam to justify a boys-only session. Camp Sunbeam has historically had far more girls than boys attending. I think at one point it may have been exclusively a girls' camp.

When I got out of my mother's car, there were plenty of other campers being unloaded. I remembered vaguely that the campers were supposed to meet in the gymnasium at a certain time. I began making my way over there. Halfway there, I got the inevitable "Have you got everything?" from my mother. I looked at my suitcase and assured her that I did have everything I meant to bring even though I could not see inside the suitcase. "Remember, if you have any problem you can go to Benjamin Heimer." She told me to have a good time and we hugged.

The time for goodbyes was over, and it was now time for hellos. I was first greeted by the mountain in the distance. It was the same mountain that I encountered upon arrival at camp the other two years I came. Despite its distance, the mountain rose impressively above everything else I could see. It had streaks and patches of snow along its peak and sub-peaks which were made of exposed stone.

I began walking towards the gym because I remembered from past years at camp that the campers gathered there upon arrival. I went inside the gym and there were campers everywhere and a few people who were old enough to be staff members or other camp workers. Slowly campers began taking seats on the floor some sitting Indian style. Finally, Benjamin Heimer got on the stage which is on the far side of the gym. "Welcome to Camp Sunbeam," his voice was full of enthusiasm.

The man continued after a pause that lasted about half a minute. "Right here we will tell you which hut you are in, and we will go outside, and I will explain the rules. Then you will go in your cabins and your leaders (that is what they call counselors at Camp Sunbeam) will help you choose and sign up for activities. We will all pitch in to make sure you understand your schedule and how to find your way around the camp."

"Right now, hut leaders will be announcing the names of those of you who have been assigned to their hut. Please come join him or her on the stage when your name is called. First, Barbara, one of the leaders in the Sioux hut, will be announcing who will be in that hut." All of the huts are named after American Indian tribes. Barbara announced the name of a little girl, and she came running up to Barbara screaming with excitement as though she cared what hut she was sent to. The Sioux appeared to be the youngest of the girls' huts. When the Sioux were all called a male counselor got the microphone and began calling boys to his hut. These boys were about the same age as the girls in the Sioux hut. As the hut leaders, one after another, called out the members of their huts, the campers got progressively older. Since I was undoubtedly in the oldest boys' hut and they were calling the huts in a girl-boy format, I was sure that whatever hut I was assigned to would be last. If *Harry Potter and the Sorcerer's Stone* was in bookstores back then and I had read it, I would have felt like I was in my first day at Hogwarts School and the sorting hat was choosing a "house" for each student.

Eventually all the girl campers had been selected by the girls' huts, and all but a few boys were called into huts. At this point they could have simply decided that all remaining boys are assigned to the Shoshone hut since there were no other huts to be sorted into, but they continued the name calling ritual. I heard them call the names of the boys in the hut I would inevitably be in including my own name. "Tom Gleason," I am not sure why my name was one of the last to be called or if there even was a reason. The hut I was called into was the Shoshone hut. I walked up to the stage to join the others. Like all the other huts, when our group was complete, we walked off the stage back to the main floor but this time we stayed close together as a group like all the other groups did.

We followed Director Heimer out of the gym and towards the area where the cabins were. One of the things he told us was this: "There is an invisible line which goes from the end of the bridge (I forgot to mention that there was a bridge across a river which separated the residential area from most of the rest of the camp) to that round building back there which is called the Rotunda. The boys have to stay on this side of the line and the girls have to stay on the other side of the line. It is very important that you follow this instruction. Your leaders will now lead you into your huts." We followed the teen that called our names in the gym as he led us to our hut.

The cabin I was assigned to was completely built of faded brown wood. All of the windows were filled with screen, not glass. In fact, almost every building at camp was like that. Stairs at the front of the hut led to a pair of front doors which were also screened and were about one and a half meters from the ground. The hut had a low angle roof.

I went inside the cabin with the other boys while I was holding my suitcase which I had actually been carrying this whole time. I claimed a bed. We then all gathered into what passed for a living room inside the hut. There were actually two leaders in our hut. One introduced himself as Bob Miles and the other introduced himself as Adam Craig.

"It is great to have all of you here," Bob began. "I love Camp Sunbeam. I love the air at Camp Sunbeam. This place has always been a great escape for me. I was here as a camper for many years. Now I would like for each of you to introduce yourselves telling us your name and then telling us something you like to do. Then tell us what all the others said was their name and what they like to do. There is only one rule. When telling us what you like to do, it can't have anything to do with girls or women."

"Why not?" the question came from one of the campers behind me.

Adam was the one to answer even though he was not the one to announce the rule. "Because it is a given that we all like women and I want to know what else you like," was his answer.

I was chosen to go first. I did not know whether to feel flattered or embarrassed, so I cooperated. "My name is Tom and I like to read books."

The second camper introduced himself as Juan and told us what he liked to do and also mentioned my name and said what I liked to do. The third camper introduced himself as Dan and his favorite activity which was playing an electric guitar and talked about the first two campers as instructed. Each camper in turn introduced himself and said what he liked to do while mentioning all the other campers who had told us about themselves. One camper whose name was Dwight told us he liked to listen to music. Another whose name was Taylor shared that he liked to play with cats (something I also happen to like to do). Another camper, Logan, said he liked to play baseball and yet another, Jacob, said he liked to fool around with girls. This drew giggles and a sharp rebuke from Adam and Bob, whom we would often call "Bobby", as well as a few campers. It gave me the impression that the real reason for this rule was to prevent such giggles. The remaining campers were Mark, Joey, Ray, Paul, Hank, Pete, Brandon, and Ryan.

When we had all introduced ourselves, Bobby began speaking. "It is great to meet all of you. I have something very important and very special to share with all of you. I will talk about it tonight. Right now, let's get ready for dinner. That is in thirty minutes."

The campers used those thirty minutes to finish organizing around their beds, trying to get to know the campers in the beds next to them, or just sitting on their beds waiting. "Gather up, it's dinner time," both Adam and Bobby seemed to say in unison. We all left the hut and walked towards the dining hall which we loved to call the mess hall. Calling it that made us feel like we were in the military. When we got to the mess hall, we coalesced into a line. There were other groups of campers both ahead of us and behind us in line. It was several minutes until the line even began to move. I didn't mind. I was at camp.

The possibilities seemed endless.

We went into the rustic building (actually all the buildings at Camp Sunbeam are rustic), picked up trays, picked up plates to put on those trays, and had food served to us onto our plates. Our hut went to two neighboring tables assigned to us. Drinks were delivered to us shortly after we sat down. When we were almost finished eating Mark put a spoon over his nose. I knew the drill. We were playing "pig." "Pig" is a game in which one camper does something odd and all other campers at that table must imitate him. The last camper to do so is designated "pig." That camper must clean up the table at the end of the meal and take all the plates back to the kitchen. Similar rounds were played for "assistant pig" and "floor cleaner." I alertly followed the lead in the first two rounds but was caught off guard the third time, so I was assigned the floors. When everybody left the table Adam gave me a broom and dustpan and I cleaned up beneath the table. "Where shall I take the dustpan?" I reluctantly accepted my role.

"Follow me."

I followed Adam to a trash can by the door we had come in through. I quickly dumped what little dust I had in the dustpan into that can. Adam took the broom and dustpan to the back of the mess hall for me. Shortly after we returned to our table in the dining area, one of the Aztecs called for our attention. The Aztecs were college aged boys who specialized in an activity and taught the campers how to do the activity. Their female counterparts were called Chippewas. This Aztec announced that our leaders would give us the opportunity to choose activities later that night but that at the meantime, we could enjoy playing whatever games we came up with in the gym.

We filed out of the mess hall and towards the gym. We picked up balls and began shooting baskets even with balls that were not basketballs. Some campers walked around the stage which was on the far side of the gym court. Some of the things we did resembled Calvinball, a game played in the comic strip *Calvin and Hobbes* by the namesake characters. This comic strip began running in *The Oregonian* my local newspaper a few months later and ran for ten years. Eventually the boys settled on playing dodgeball which we called "warball." The girls coalesced on the other end of the gym and played basketball.

Shortly after we returned to our hut, our leaders asked us to sign up for activities. Adam got with me with a piece of paper on a clipboard and worked with me to pick out activities. My first task was to pick out an activity for Session One. A column just to the right of each session indicated what "period" the session took place in. The "periods" were numbered. It made me feel like I was picking classes for high school since it also had numbered periods. The next column told what days and times the period took place. Finally, there was a column with the activities available for that session. The activities had oval bubbles by them to fill out just like those achievement tests we took at school every year. I chose canoeing for Session One. I just wouldn't feel like I was at camp if I didn't take canoeing.

For Session Two, I chose "Arts and Craft." Frankly, this seemed like it would be a boring activity and I don't really remember why I chose it. Session Three: "Games." Session Four: Archery. Two types of games were available for Session Five: tennis and "Gym Games". I remember taking tennis the previous year. A boy behind me being guided to the activity by one of the Aztecs was for some reason forced to play tennis. This boy was constantly getting into trouble. He was complaining the whole way about having to play tennis. "Whoever invented tennis must have been gay." This was the last straw. The Aztec then grabbed him almost by the ear and took him away to wherever campers go when they are in trouble. Obviously, I didn't agree with that camper. I had chosen to take tennis. This year, however, I chose to find out what "Gym Games" meant. I wondered what games we would play. In retrospect maybe they called it "Gym Games" instead of just "Gym" to reassure campers that it would not be like gym class at school, and they would not have to do jumping jacks or anything like that.

Swimming was the only formally required activity at Camp Sunbeam, but we had flexibility as to when we could take it. I chose to do it in Session 6.

I eyed riflery for Session 7. This sport was restricted to campers at least 13 years old and required parental permission. This is the first year my mother gave me permission to take riflery.

Save the best for last. At least that was the opinion of Camp Sunbeam. For the eighth and final session I chose horseback riding. Everyone at Camp Sunbeam took horseback riding. I was handed the schedule I filled out. I was all set.

The interior of the cabin had a different feel at night. There was no light except the harsh cream light coming from the incandescent light bulbs in circular cages hanging from the ceiling.

Bobby gathered us at one end of the hut and spoke to us. "It is good to have all of you here." Bobby continued. "I wanted to tell you something important about myself and Camp Sunbeam. This is a Christian camp. Camp Sunbeam is financed and operated by various Christian denominations. That's a fancy way of saying that many different kinds of Christians give money to the camp and help run it. Both Christians and non-Christians are welcome here at Camp Sunbeam. Can anyone here tell me what a Christian is?"

Juan raised his hand to volunteer to answer the question. When Bob called on him, Juan answered, "A Christian is someone who believes that Jesus Christ is the Son of God."

"Very good. A Christian also believes that God offers salvation to us through Jesus. Some people think that a Christian is someone who prays and reads the Bible. That's not true. That is how the world sees a Christian. You may want to ask me what you must do to get into heaven. I don't blame you. That is a very important question. The truth is that we can never do enough good deeds to get into heaven. While the price of sin may be too high for any of us to pay, Jesus paid that price for us. The offer of salvation and eternal life is there but we have to accept it."

"Our mission at Camp Sunbeam is not to get you to become Christians. It is to tell you of what it means to be a Christian so that you can make an informed choice of whether or not Christianity is for you. Jesus means a lot to me. I invite all of you to use your time here to think about what, if anything, Jesus means to you."

"Lights out is in," Bobby then looked at his wristwatch, "about twenty minutes." I sat on my cot thinking about all of what he had taught us. I had long wondered what I would experience when I died. I was ashamed of the way I acted when I was a younger child. Of course, I was younger back then and God would understand. At this point in my life, I had matured into a better person. Still, I wondered if it was enough. I had volunteered for charity work a few times and had given money to charity for starving people in Africa but was not sure I was good enough to go to heaven. I certainly didn't want to go to the other place. Finally, I decided to walk into the small room where Bobby slept.

"Can I talk to you?" Bobby then led me out to the front steps of our cabin.

"I was just thinking about what you were saying," I continued, "and I'm glad Jesus went through all that for me, but…"

Bobby gently interrupted. "I am going to ask you something and I want you to be totally honest with me. If you were to die tonight, what do you think would happen to you?"

"Well, I think I would go to heaven but I'm not sure."

"What if I were to tell you that there is a way you can be sure?"

"I don't know."

"You can get assurance of eternal life in heaven. God offers salvation to you through Jesus. All you have to do is accept. Do you want to accept the salvation of Jesus?"

"Certainly."

Bobby leaned into me and took my hand. He then said this prayer after instructing me to repeat after him. "Lord, I am sorry for my sins. I accept the salvation you offer me through your Son Jesus Christ. Please guide me as I follow the teachings of your Son. This I pray in His name. Amen."

Then Bobby let go of my hand and began praying on his own. "Yes, please guide this new follower of your Son and assure Tom that there is eternal life for him. This I pray in Jesus' name. Amen."

After this I felt renewed. Suddenly it didn't matter what I had done in the past, at least not eternally. Jesus had wiped the slate clean. I had been told that I was baptized as a baby but of course I was too young to remember it. I had even been confirmed in my family's church at the age of twelve, but I didn't really know what was going on. Our family's attendance at that church was at best intermittent. This time it was different. It was sincere, conscious, and with an adequate understanding of the decision I made. For many years I would tell people that a camp counselor led me to Christ.

Chapter Three

Sunday, June 30, 1985

We would all like to have been woken up by Reveille. It would have played into our fantasy about being in the military. But it wasn't that dramatic. Instead, Bobby came in and pretended to be a disc jockey for a radio station. He announced the call letters of a radio station I didn't recognize and gave a weather report. Some of us were already awake. After Bobby's wakeup call, some campers began conversing. Thirty minutes later we were all dressed and ready to go to breakfast.

I basked in the fresh morning air, felt fresh, more tranquil because of my new faith, and ready to enjoy the day. Along the way I felt sure that I had seen a beautiful diagonal column of sunshine highlighted by dust. *Maybe that's why they call it Camp Sunbeam.* We did not play "pig" at breakfast perhaps because they did not expect everyone to be fully awake and alert.

When we returned to our hut from breakfast, we were told that we would have a drama period and we needed to come up with skits to perform on the gymnasium stage. Juan offered a suggestion. "I have an idea. We can do a skit about an 'all you can eat' diner. Actually, it will mean 'all you can eat until you throw up.' The plot is simple. A man comes into this diner and eats and tries to walk away but he is told that the sign means 'all you can eat,' not 'all you want to eat.' Then two muscular men come along and force him to stay seated and then start force feeding him until he throws up."

"Sounds like a good one," Adam approved.

I also had a suggestion. "How 'bout a skit like *Miami Vice*. Only it would be called 'Sunbeam Vice.' It could be about people who get Oasis treats before lunch."

Oasis was a store at camp which sold soft drinks and candy. It was only open for about thirty minutes and some of the huts would be taken there by their leaders so that campers could buy snacks. I think it was also open at a later time for the huts with younger campers. Oasis also had a few non-food items such as T-shirts with the camp's name on it. Having Oasis before was obviously forbidden. Camp Sunbeam staff members were always threatening campers with "no Oasis" for the day. I think they had Oasis to have something they could take away from us if we were bad.

My "Sunbeam Vice" idea was accepted. Bobby then asked for more ideas from the hut.

Discussion led to a third idea. There would be a skit about a magician putting on a magic show who would try to turn an egg into a full-grown chicken. The magician would literally get egg on his face. The idea came from Hank who performed magic shows as a hobby and felt like he was a natural fit for the role.

Another skit would be about a piece of bubble gum which was used by multiple people.

"Who wants to do the 'all you can eat' skit?" Adam needed volunteers. There were six volunteers for this. Although this skit was not my idea, I was one of the volunteers. "We really only need four. "Two of the campers who had volunteered agreed to consider the other skits. Then Adam wrote our names on a notepad. "Who wants to do 'Sunbeam Vice'?" I was honored to have four campers want to volunteer for the act that was a creation of my mind. This included one of the campers who initially wanted to do "All You Can Eat."

"How many of you are not in a skit so far?" Bobby was making sure nobody was left out. Seven hands went up. "Four of you can be in the 'Bubble Gum' skit. Hank, the other two can act as audience members for your magic show." Two campers joined Hank's skit.

"You, you, you, and you will be in 'Bubble Gum,'" Adam was pointing in succession to the campers who had not been recruited into any of the other three acts.

With the casting for the four skits set, our leaders moved on to the joint performance. It was clear that since we had to spend so much time learning and practicing the skits and with short notice, the best idea for the joint act would be a song. "Is everybody familiar with 'We Are the World'?" Adam was considering the possibility that some campers may not know everything about it. "Does everybody know the lyrics? If not, that's okay because the song will be playing in the background, and you can pretend to be singing along and they won't notice."

"We Are the World" was a contemporary popular music song performed jointly by numerous rock, pop, and country artists. The proceeds for the album it was on went to world hunger charities. For about a year, some parts of Africa had been suffering from a catastrophic famine. I had heard some stories about the desperate things people there did to stay alive and relieve the agony of hunger which almost brought tears to my eyes immediately and even gave me a few nightmares. Some of the kids at my school thought the song was not well done. Others were tired of it.

"I'll be Michael Jackson."

"I'll be Stevie Wonder."

Our two leaders never mentioned any requirement that we be specific singers but that didn't stop my hut mates from claiming these roles. The important thing is that nobody in our cabin objected to doing this song and even if there had been a few such campers, the song could have still been done without them.

"'Sunbeam Vice', over here," Bobby instructed. "I'll arrange for some music. Meanwhile, you and you," while pointing to campers doing 'Sunbeam Vice', "be the traders in the illegal deal. "Logan, Paul," while talking about the other two campers in that group, "Run up to them right after something appears to change hands and use your fingers as guns for the raid."

Paul agreed to say, "Oasis before lunch is the disease. We're the cure."

"I like that," Logan described it as "cool."

The leaders then turned their attention to the 'bubble gum' skit and helped them with their plot. "You know that actual bubble gum is against camp policy," Bobby reminded them. "You can use some other object, or you can just pretend to have some gum. Since you are actually putting it in your mouth in this story, I suggest the latter." After helping them rehearse very briefly (we had very little time), he asked Hank if he had all that he needed for his magic show. Bobby mentioned that he would have to hope the mess hall would give him some eggs.

Finally, he got around to our little play about the "all you can eat" customer. I was chosen to be one of the big muscular men who would hold the customer in place.

Once the mental scripts were settled for all these skits and it was decided who was in what acting role, the leaders instructed us to keep practicing until time to leave the cabin.

It seemed only a short time until we heard "time to go now." We all got in a line and filed out of the hut.

The first act was done by the youngest boys' hut. As we were seated on the floor, the boys on stage all stood by each other and sang "This Land is Your Land."

Next a young girls' hut performed a skit in which the girls took on the roles of vegetables and three of them identified themselves by vegetable.

"I'm a stalk of corn and I grow in the Midwest. I'm also rich in fiber and protein."

"I'm a carrot and I help people see in the dark."

"I'm a potato and I'm full of starch."

Broccoli, green peas, cabbage, onions, and tomatoes were also represented.

"We know each other well but we don't really know any people," Broccoli Girl commented.

"Why don't people know about us?" Carrot Girl had an important question.

"Maybe they just avoid us because they think we are yucky." This reply came from Tomato Girl. "Actually, we are delicious and good for people. We just need to get the word out on us. Onion, I know you make people cry but if they knew how good you were for them, they would be happy instead. Here come some people right now. Let's go meet them." The few remaining girls who were not vegetables came out onto the stage and the vegetable girls approached them.

Tomato Girl introduced herself and the other vegetables to the non-vegetable girls. "We have a lot to tell you about us. Let's go for a walk and we can get to know each other," Tomato Girl continued as they walked off stage. A moment later, all the girls came out. Broccoli Girl had the heavy responsibility of giving the final spoken line. "Be sure to eat and meet your vegetables."

A boys' hut replaced the girls on the stage and performed a skit based on *The Goonies,* a movie that was in theaters at the time and which I had seen just a few days before. They used the second half of their allotted time for a political satire which was probably copied from or at least inspired by *Saturday Night Live.* Next was a girls' hut which performed several parodies of television commercials.

Then it was our turn. I had the privilege of being in the first skit. There was a desk on stage resembling one that a student uses at school. One of us sat in it.

"That was great," the boy in the desk pretended to comment on the food (which wasn't really there) after briefly pretending to eat. "Can I get my check."

"Actually, no. Do you see that sign up there? It says 'all you can eat,' not 'all you want to eat.' We are going to see how much you can eat before you throw up."

Juan and I walked forward and held the boy at the desk in place. Another one of us pretended to bring more food. We even pretended to force feed him. Then we walked off stage and back into the audience.

Other Shoshones (reminder: That is our hut name.) came onto the stage and Phil Collins' "In the Air Tonight" began playing. Two Shoshones started stealthily walking towards each other. When they reached each other, they pretended to exchange something. Immediately after this "exchange", the music stopped. Then Paul and Logan ran onto the stage screaming "BUST" and using their fingers as guns. All the boys then faced the stage and Paul, one of the two "cops," told the audience "Oasis before lunch is the disease. We're the cure."

The actors cleared the stage and immediately Brandon came on stage. He was pretending to chew gum. "I'm tired of this bubble gum." Then he pretended to put bubble gum on a post that had been put on stage.

As he walked offstage, Mark walked onstage. "Somebody left some bubble gum here. Let me see if it's any good." He then pretended to take it off the post, chew it, and put it back on the post. "It's out of flavor now." He then pretended to place the gum back on the post and walked offstage.

Ray walked onstage and pretended to sneeze into his hands. He then pretended to take the gum off the post and be the third boy chew it. "Yuk!" Like the other two boys, he pretended to put it back on the post and walked offstage.

Brandon, who was the first to put the gum on that post, walked back onstage. "I'm glad my bubble gum is still here. I think I want to chew it some more." He pretended to take it off the post and chew it while walking offstage.

Various campers in the audience were saying things like "ooooh" and "gross."

The post was removed from the stage and a table was put onstage. Then Hank walked up to the table. Hank placed the hat he had been wearing and showed the audience an actual egg he had in his hand. "Eggs are supposed to grow up to be chickens. Right?" Hank explained. "With magic I can turn this egg into a live chicken instantly." Hank put the magic top hat he had been wearing on the table. He then put the egg in the hat and waved a magic wand over the hat while saying what were supposed to be magic words. "I will now put this hat on top of my head and a chicken will fly out." Hank did so. "Now when I take off my …" Hank was interrupted because egg yolk began to come out of the hat and down his face. The three boys who served as his onstage audience in chairs clapped sarcastically. The failure was intentional. It drew plenty of laughs from the offstage audience. I had to give credit to Hank for being willing to endure the discomfort of literally having egg on his face.

A moment after the stage was cleared, we all came out and lined up at the front of the stage standing side by side. "We Are the World" began playing. A moment later the lyrics started, and we began singing. Actually, most of that song was one person singing at a time. We sang our parts in turn. We were aided, of course, by the fact that the song with the original singers singing was being played. We got applause when the song was over, and we walked offstage.

The Teninos, the oldest girls' hut, were next. Some of the girls sat around in a relaxed fashion onstage. Soon it became obvious they were pretending to lounge around in their hut. "You, know. I hate that ridiculous line between us and the guys' hut," one of the girls complained or was at least acting as a complainer. "We can't see those cute Cayuses." The Cayuse hut was boys' hut whose members were on average only slightly younger than us. *Don't you mean "those cute Shoshones?"*

"Yeah, what a bummer," another one of the girls chimed in. "Like what are we supposed to do all day?"

"Nothing to do?" a third girl added a different perspective. "Are you kidding? We have tons of activities set up for us here at Camp Sunbeam."

The first girl to complain seemed to have a change of heart. "I guess it doesn't matter that there's a line. Just as long as God is pleased with how we are living." The girls cleared the stage and other Teninos went onstage. These new girls on the stage seemed to be trying to be as masculine in appearance, clothes, and demeanor as possible.

"It sure is tough being a guy during coed camp," one of these girls began the acting with a terribly fake masculine voice. "It makes me feel so self-conscious and I don't know how to impress the girls."

"Me too," another girl agreed. Two other girls did not speak but nodded in agreement.

"Let's get together and talk about how we can impress not only the girls but people in general here at camp." All of the girls, who again were pretending to be guys, huddled together and seemed to be whispering. Then they broke huddle and one of them grabbed an actual boom box (this was slang for a large portable radio than can also play cassette tapes) and put on sunglasses and put the boom box to her ear. She walked forward while at the same time dancing very poorly.

Another girl took off her Seattle Mariners cap and put it back on backwards. Then she spit on the floor and dropped a crumpled piece of paper.

"Hey, foul ball!" What Joey thought was out of bounds was the ridicule these girls seemed to be directing towards our hut. When I turned and looked at Joey, he turned his head towards me as well. "We're not like that and they know it." This was the last act of the entire camp talent show and I hated that it ended on such a divisive note.

When we got back to our cabin, Joey continued complaining about the mocking he thought we were getting from the Tenino girls.

A few of us agreed that the act was an unfair portrayal of our hut. Fellow Shoshone Ray Schmitz, on the other hand, asked Joey how he could be so sure it was about us.

"Think about it," Joey answered. "We have radios visible in these screen windows. One of those girls made a snide comment about our table in the mess hall yesterday."

"Hey, Cyndi Lauper," Mark called out from a distance. "Don't worry about it." Cyndi Lauper was the pop singer whose part Joey sang in the "We Are the World" performance. After this, the nickname stuck. From then on, Joey was called "Cyndi Lauper" by all of the other Shoshones including me.

I made my way from our hut to the creek for canoeing. There was a section of Jasmine's Creek that was so wide it almost deserved to be called a lake. From there, Jasmine Creek narrowed and there was a rocky waterfall. The canoes were on the shore of this wide part of the creek. We were each assigned one canoe mate. I was assigned to canoe with Pete, and I launched the canoe from the shore and we both rowed. "Stop sloshing me," Pete complained. I continued paddling the best that I could in the best way I knew how. As we got away from the shore and out into the open, the canoe seemed peaceful. That peace was shattered by more complaints from Pete. "You obviously don't know how to canoe," he was still irritated. I really didn't see anything wrong with the way I was paddling.

"We are not even going in the right direction," Pete would not stop berating me. What was the right direction anyway? We were following the other canoers ahead of us. Maybe that was his point. We were behind all of the others. I didn't think it mattered where we went just as long as we didn't go towards the waterfall. "Paddle deeper," Pete tried to instruct me. We got closer to the other canoes over time. The most difficult task was turning around to go back to the point on the shore where we first got in the canoes. All of the other canoes were turning around, and I assumed that we were being instructed to do so. I was having a hard enough time having Pete as a canoe mate. I felt like I didn't need the added difficulty of turning the canoe.

Pete instructed me on the turnaround. This time his tone was gentler, and his instructions were detailed. We succeeded in turning around. Once we were going straight, Pete continued his verbal lashing. "You're still getting water on me." Finally, I asked him to show me exactly how to paddle. Pete then made a stroke with his paddle in slow motion. I resumed paddling trying my best to paddle the way he showed me, but he still criticized me. "You have obviously never done this before." That was not true. I had done canoeing my previous two years at Camp Sunbeam. In my own mind, however, I admitted to myself that there were probably others here at camp, possibly including

Pete, who were much more experienced at canoeing than I was.

Mercifully we reached the original canoe launching shore. As soon as we both got out, Pete wasted no time in telling me this. "I'm never going canoeing with you again."

"Maybe there was something wrong with the paddle," I responded.

"It's you."

Pete then walked away unhappy. In retrospect I would like to have told him that maybe he would be happier canoeing with someone with more experience. At the time, however, it was very hard not to take it personally.

When we returned to the hut, those of us who had gone canoeing got out of our bathing suits and not only put on different clothes but put on our better clothes. Why? Because the girls were coming. Although the boys and girls were in huts on opposite sides of a line and we were required to stay on our side of that line, a visitation period in which the girls could visit boys' huts was scheduled. Some girls from the Tenino hut knocked on the door of our hut and came in immediately.

We were ready.

Chapter Four

The girls all introduced themselves. Their names were Kelly, Rita, Holly, Allison, and Karen. Some but not all of the boys in our hut met and visited with these girls in the part of the hut that was the closest thing the cabin had to a living room. I was one of the boys in there with the girls, but I was not very involved in the conversation.

The way the conversation started was unfortunate. "I didn't like that act of yours," Cyndi Lauper began the exchange. "You made us look stupid when we aren't."

"If you will look around, you will see that our hut is clean," Mark added.

Rita then admitted that the skit was indeed about us. "We're sorry," she concluded.

"We really don't think you guys are that bad," Kelly assured us. "That was actually my jam box that was being used. I brought it to camp so I can listen to Lionel Richie. I went to one of his concerts in Seattle." I was glad to hear the conversation drifting away from the skit that made fun of us.

"Is that where you're from?" Mark was curious.

"Yeah. Actually, I'm from all over. I'm in one of those military families that moves around a lot."

"Have you seen any good movies lately?" Taylor seemed to want the conversation to continue to drift to small talk.

"*I* have," Allison answered even though Taylor seemed to be talking to Kelly. "*The Goonies* was great. In fact, I live about a mile from where they filmed it."

"I loved it when the man on the toilet was pushed up to the ceiling," Rita referred to one of the movie's many funny scenes. The conversation continued about movies and later we talked about other things such as school and school lunches. I remained silent throughout the conversation.

Later after the girls had left, I heard an interesting song. Ray Schmitz played a song on his boom box by the rap band Run DMC. It started with "Shut up!" It continued with "You talk too much. You never shut up." Other lyrics included "You talk about your girl from head to toe," and "25 hours a day, eight days a week." This last lyric was apparently describing how much the subject talked. Several other campers in my hut had radios and jam boxes.

Later I went to my least favorite activity: Craft. I didn't hate the activity. It is just that if I were surveyed on my favorite activities in order of preference, this would be at the bottom. Why? Because it took me a while to catch onto a project, but when I did catch on, I was fine. I arrived at a small open-air hut with tables and places to sit. We were given paint and plates, the kind of plates used for meals. They told us we were welcome to take the plates home and use them there. I got to work thinking of what to paint on my plate. "What kinds of things do you paint on a plate?" I was hoping Rita, the Chippewa on the scene, could help me with ideas.

"Whatever you want," she answered cheerfully. "If you want some ideas, the younger campers who were here earlier painted things like flowers, trees, houses, dogs, and sometimes people."

After hearing that, however, I decided to paint something different. I began the work of painting a jet fighter airplane on my plate. Ray Schmitz was the only camper from my hut at Craft. "Its three o'clock right now. *Voltron* is on. That's a cartoon I watch on TV when I have nothing else to do."

"I like *The Superfriends,*" I added.

"Oh, that's old," Rita sneered. "Nobody watches that anymore."

"Sometimes we watch cartoons, but we also like to play hopscotch, write things on the sidewalk," one of two girls sitting together joined the conversation. "Those are things we like to do in Lakota. That's the name of the town we're from."

I naturally turned my head to these girls when one of them spoke. She seemed to be talking to all of us but when I was looking her way, the girl spoke directly to me.

"I'm Isabella," she introduced herself and as she casually put her hand behind the other girl she continued, "and this is my best friend, Stacy."

"I'm Tom." Both girls were about a year or two younger than me.

Although Craft was my least favorite activity, once I spent some time on a project and was successful, I got some measure of enjoyment from it. I finished painting the airplane on my plate and added a sun for good measure. At the end of the Craft session, a boy about my age approached Isabella. "Oh hey, Thomas," Isabella greeted him. There are two reasons I knew she was not talking to me but rather to the boy who had just arrived. The first reason is that she was facing him, not me. Second, even though my name is Thomas, I was usually called Tom. Today family and close friends still call me "Tom." Thomas and Isabella left together walking very close to each other.

I walked alone to another activity.

I arrived at a clearing where the Games activity would take place. Several other campers were already there as well as a young man who was obviously the Aztec on the scene. After a few more campers arrived, he introduced himself as Chris and told us to line up in a straight line. Then Chris walked in front of the line we formed alternately saying "A" and "B." Soon after Chris finished this, we understood why he did it. "If I said 'A' when I pointed at you, you are on Team A. The rest of you are on Team B." I was glad he did it this way because it spared me the agony of the picking teams ritual. We often did it that way at physical education class at school and I was usually the last or second last to be picked.

We were told we were playing kickball. I was on Team B, and I got together with the other Team B members. We were kicking first. Chris explained that since "B" was not first in the alphabet, that it should be the first team to kick. Our first kicker kicked it hard. The ball was caught by the shortstop who threw it to first base. He missed our kicker and the infielder at first base wildly. "Go, Mike," I heard one of my teammates say. Mike made it to third base before the other team got the ball and forced him to stop running. Some of the players, including the next kicker, were girls. This girl kicked it lightly and started running towards first base. "No bunts," one of the fielders yelled. It worked like a bunt is supposed to. The roller quickly picked up the ball, threw it at our kicker successfully hitting her with the ball so she was out. However, Mike made it to home plate for our first run. What is interesting here is that Chris, who was for all practical purposes our P. E. coach, did not make any rules. We did, and we made them as the game was being played. The bunt ban we agreed on here was only one example. There was, however, one time Chris intervened. Later when we were fielding, one of the other team's kickers told our roller to roll it slowly. Several other kickers on their team and ours had asked the roller to roll the ball a particular way.

"What's the matter with you guys?" Chris seemed appalled. "You don't get what kind of pitch you want in baseball."

A lot of runs were scored in the game. They were mostly the result of fielders trying to hit base runners with the ball and missing. In some cases, the ball would roll far away after missing the runner. My team was actually up 10-0 at the end of the first half of the first inning. In the bottom half of the inning, Team A made the score 10-6. After two innings Chris announced, "We will play one more inning. One of our biggest players opened the third inning with a home run, the first of the game. With a runner on third base this gave us two runs 16-19 with our team trailing. We scored six more runs to make it 22-19 before three of us were out. When the other team was kicking in the bottom half of the third and last inning, we did a great job of defense. Why? It occurred to us that we should be throwing the ball at our basemen (and base women since some of our players were girls) instead of at the other team's base runners. Plus, we were trying harder since the game depended on how we did in this half inning.

Soon there were two outs but two was also the number of runs Team A had scored. They also had a runner on third. We couldn't screw this up. We had to hope to catch the ball in the air when kicked or that they would make a poor and light kick and we could put out either the runner headed home or the one going towards first base. The next roll seemed much slower than it actually was. It was one of those classic "hold your breath" moments in sports. The Team A kicker kicked it hard, and the ball went a long way. Our outfielder ran back to catch the ball. I was encouraged that she slowed down because that meant that she was in position to catch the ball. The outfielder was at the edge of the clearing when she caught the ball. This ended the game. Our team cheered the victory while running off the field.

While we were running, we heard a voice say, "You guys lost. You caught it out of bounds." We slowed down and gathered around Chris. The boy speaking continued to make his point. "It was a home run. Therefore, we won 23 to 22."

The girl who caught it for our team countered with the argument, "If there had actually been a wall there it would have bounced off the wall and I would have caught it."

I stood and listened to the debate not because I had a strongly felt opinion about who won but because I was intrigued by the argument. A few others hung around too and occasionally joined the argument but most of the campers left so they could go to other activities. It seemed like Chris would have tried to settle the dispute, but he didn't. When I was walking back towards the hut, one of the campers turned to me hoping I could confirm something for him. "We won. Didn't we?"

"Yeah," I absentmindedly answered.

The game, however, was not mentioned again in my hut even though many of the players on both teams were in my hut.

I stopped by the hut, asked Bobby for directions to the archery field, and went there.

Archery took place in a clearing. There were four target boards and plenty of arrows. The arrows were very sharp. Logically I should have not been surprised that they were sharp. Bows were weapons of war for a long time until they became obsolete. But for some reason I never thought of them as being sharp. Although the age restriction was not as high as the limit for riflery, it was an age restricted activity.

The Chippewa on the scene introduced herself as Millie. "How many of you have never ever shot a bow and arrow?" Almost every camper on the scene, including me, raised their hands. "It's really simple." Despite Millie's words shooting an arrow appeared, based on the demonstration she did for us, a little more complicated than I imagined. "When it's your turn to shoot, come up here with a bow and four arrows," Millie instructed us while pointing to a pile of bows and arrows.

There were four round targets, the kind traditionally used in archery. One camper at a time shot at each target. When it was my turn, I picked up a bow and four arrows as instructed and walked up to a newly vacant spot for shooting. We all had to stay behind a white powder line. Millie worked closely with me to help me pair the arrow with the bow and shoot. When she had me ready, she told me to let go of the bow. The arrow landed in the grass slightly short and slightly wide of the target stand. When Millie handed me another arrow, I shook it in frustration.

"If you are going to get angry, you can leave," she warned me. I was embarrassed at how bad I was at archery. I was already frustrated. If I couldn't hit the bull's eye, I felt like I should at least hit the target. Then I saw another camper shoot and hit the target, but it was on the edge of the target; she almost missed the entire target. This made me feel better. The other archers were apparently not much better than me. I shot my next arrow and had the same result. It was a few minutes until I had another turn at shooting. When it came, I allowed Millie to help me up close. I had to put the arrow in just the right position within the bow. Only after carefully positioning myself and the arrow did I actually pull back and let go. I did not even come close to hitting the bull's eye, but it was better than my previous shot. The remainder of the shots I took either hit moderately close-in or hit close to the edge, but all at least hit the target. In retrospect not bad for a beginner.

After archery I walked back to our hut. It was a strange feeling to be walking from one place to another at camp. I felt so independent. I liked it. It was something I had not experienced before except at camp. I went from class to class in high school, but this felt different. It was probably because I was living at camp. I slept there overnight and the place I was going to *was* my "home." At least it was for that week.

At dinner when we were almost finished eating, Brandon who was sitting at our table left the table, picked up a jug from another table, and put it on top of his head. This was part of playing "pig."

"No pig where you have to leave the table," a camp staff member ordered.

A moment later Brandon put his glass of tea by his right ear. Everyone at our table did the same thing. Ray, the last to get his glass up to his ear, became assistant pig. When we were almost finished eating dinner, Brandon put his napkin over his lower face. He looked like a bandit. The others at the table followed suit. I was caught off guard and didn't do it. "You do the floors," Brandon instructed while pointing gently as me. It seemed that I always ended up sweeping the floors. I didn't mind so much helping out with the cleaning after a meal. I just hated that I always got the same chore almost every meal. I decided that at our next meal, I would volunteer to be assistant pig or lose on purpose just to avoid being assigned to the floors.

I had to ask Adam where I could get a broom and dustpan. He went back into the kitchen and came back with them. There wasn't much under the table. I had to hold the broom at a low angle which was difficult. Nonetheless I managed to sweep up the dust and trash beneath the table. When I was done, I emptied the dustpan into a trash can and returned it and the broom to the kitchen staff. Then I returned to my hut.

One hour after dinner our hut went to the swimming pool. After a full day of camping this felt great. The sun had not even set when we were in the pool. It was one of the longest daylight days of the year. I got into plenty of splash wars with the others in the pool. We started heading back to the hut at around 9:30 in the evening. It was finally getting dark. We were given the opportunity to shower off in the bath-house near our hut. A half hour later we were all back in the hut and in our pajamas. I ended the day entertained and refreshed.

Chapter Five

Monday, July 1, 1985

I woke up to a new day, a new month, and a new half of the year. When we were at breakfast that morning and we were playing "pig," I announced "I volunteer" when they were competing to see who would be "assistant pig." When we were all finished eating, I helped the "pig" take all the dishes to the table by loading them into a giant tray he had brought to the table. We dusted off the table one last time and were on our way back to the cabin.

Later we went from the cabin to a deck by the river for a devotional assembly. There would be a spiritual message. The beautiful, serene, natural scenery added to the spiritual experience. One of the camp staffers spoke in front of the assembly.

"I hope you are all having a nice day," he began. "It is a beautiful day out here."

Then he began the main body of his message. "I just wanted to share some thoughts about how God sees you. We think of Him as some far off being in a heavenly throne. That is certainly not how God thinks of you. Try to imagine God being interested in you and wanting to be a part of your life. Actually, I know it is just about impossible to imagine that. The best I can do is to give you examples. Wouldn't you be excited, for example, if President Reagan took an interest in your life and wanted to know more about you? We all know that is very unlikely. He's too busy. That is not a problem with God. He wants to be a part of your life and would love to learn more about you. Actually, God knows all about you, but He is also interested in you and wants to be with you in everything you are trying to do."

"If you make the basketball team, God is right there applauding you. If you are giving a piano recital, God is in the audience and He is just as excited to see you play as your parents are, actually more. God is interested in your life. If that doesn't excite you, I don't know what will." The sound of the nearby water, the gentle rays of the sun, and the quiet of the trees all added to the spiritual experience. Then we began a song led by one of the Aztecs with a guitar.

Lord, you are more precious than silver
Lord, you are more costly than gold
Lord, you are more beautiful than diamonds
And nothing I desire compares with you

It is a song that I love to this day. I thought about those who are obsessed with the silver, gold, and diamonds mentioned in the song and therefore felt a lot of frustration in life. I felt sorry for them and wished that they could have the peace of knowing these things would be provided for them.

We sang two more religious songs, both of which were fun and lighthearted in nature. Then the meeting was over, and we quietly returned to our huts.

Next up was canoeing. I changed into my bathing suit and put on moccasins but kept the same shirt on. Then I went to the canoe launching point. This time I was one of eight boys on a single canoe. Four of us had paddles, two boys on one side and two boys on the other. That left four of us including me without a paddle. I felt bad about not contributing but I was simply not one of the boys who picked up a paddle. The others got to the paddles before I did. After we had been out on the water about ten minutes, I noticed one of the guys paddling was getting tired, and I offered to take over for him. He gladly gave me the paddle.

I began to paddle the water. This time nobody criticized me. It certainly was not the nightmare that my first canoeing trip was. Pete was not on the boat and even if he was, it is unlikely, with eight of us on board, that he would have noticed how well or poorly I was paddling.

I was able to enjoy the exploring involved in going down the creek and the new and pretty scenery even when I was using the paddle. Eventually we turned around and headed back to where we launched.

I don't know why it happened. It may have been boredom, or it may have been because the other canoe came so close to ours. But it happened. It started when one of the riders of the other canoe used a paddle not for its intended purpose but to splash water on our canoe. We of course retaliated. We sent water back to the other canoe not with one but two paddles. In fact, people on my side of the boat gave their paddles to some of those on the other side so four paddles could be used in this battle. They did the same thing and some of their crew began using their hands to splash water on us. As the splashes got higher, I noticed something and pointed it out to the others. Almost directly over us hanging from a tree that leaned over the creek from the bank was a wasp nest. Some of the splashes had come dangerously close to the nest.

After a cease fire that lasted less than a minute, they began assaulting our canoe with splashes. "We need to get out of here," I was stating the obvious. We began using our paddles to get out from beneath the wasp nest.

Too late.

Just as we were a few meters farther from the nest, wasps began streaming out of the nest and flying around it. Ten seconds later they were flying farther from it, some of them halfway between the nest and the creek. The other canoe also had the good sense to be moving away from the nest. Then there were two wasps over our canoe. We paddled furiously. I picked up a paddle and helped. I was too busy paddling trying to put as much distance between the wasps and their nest as possible. Finally, the others stopped paddling and I assumed it was okay for me to do the same. I looked up and around. There were no wasps above us or anywhere near us. Their nest was barely visible in the distance, and I could not see any wasps in that direction either. They were either not present or too small to see from our distance.

I began wondering if I should grow up to be a navy captain. I had taken leadership of a boat and led a crew to safety. Later someone else on board took leadership on another issue. "Let's rock this boat," one of my canoe mates suggested when were around 100 meters from our original launching point. Canoe riders on both sides began pushing on the edge of the canoe. We were now rocking back and forth.

"It would be a shame if we did not capsize," another rider on our canoe mischievously commented on the situation. Shaking became more intense. We came closer and closer to our goal each time we rocked the canoe until finally we capsized. Like all the other passengers, I went through the sensation of splashing into the creek though I was kept afloat literally by my orange life jacket. Some of us cheered. We carried the canoe the short distance to shore. We all, of course, had to shower before going to our next activity.

Later back at the hut, one of the Aztecs paid us a visit to gauge our interest in camping out. The guys in our hut responded with comments like "That's stupid," "are you crazy," and "boring."

I, on the other hand, told the Aztec that I would love to camp out. Finally, another camper in our hut agreed to camp out. The campout was to take place tonight. The Aztec departed.

Something funny happened later during that rest period in the hut. At least I thought it was funny at the time. While Ray had Prince's "Raspberry Beret" playing on his boom box, Bobby picked it up and took it away. "No way," Ray protested.

"This is a rest period, not a listening to music period," Bobby responded. "Don't you remember us saying that we were going to start actually resting during rest period?"

"But I don't want my radio taken away."

"Obey and it might help."

When the time came to do so, I left the residential hut and arrived at the craft hut. This time the idea was to make something out of popsicle sticks. We were given such sticks and glue to work with. As with my last craft activity, I had to spend some time deciding what to make. I had to hope that when I decided, there would still be enough time left in the craft period to actually build it.

As a sixteen-year-old, I did not want anything too babyish. It did not take me long to think of and decide on an idea. When I saw several popsicle sticks lined up together parallel, it was the shape of a sled. It was a great idea. Sledding is enjoyed by kids but also by people of all ages. Portland does not get a whole lot of snow even though it is pretty far north. When it did snow, I loved to grab the sled in my bedroom closet, find a slope, and ride it down that slope. I loved the sensation. *Now is not the time to become nostalgic about winter.* I wanted to make the most of my time at camp. Nonetheless that meant taking advantage of a good idea that came to me and making a miniature sled.

The top of the sled was simple enough. I could glue six sticks together parallel. But a sled has runners underneath it, the parts of the sled that actually touch the ground. From my experience with actual sleds, two runners were sufficient for a basic sled. I just needed two popsicle sticks for that. Somehow, I had to attach it to the top. With only popsicle sticks, glue, and paint, all I could think of was to break a small piece off a popsicle stick and glue those pieces between the runners and the main body of the sled. Breaking off pieces this small was tricky. I had to put the popsicle stick on the table with the small end I wanted broken off hanging off the table. I repeated this with three other sticks. Then I glued them between the runners and the sled surface.

While I was working on this, I overheard a conversation nearby. A girl who looked to be about eleven years old casually chimed in, "This craft hut is getting to be my hangout. Actually, I don't have a hangout at home. Do you?"

She was talking to Stacy and Isabella. "We like to hang out at the Hardee's in our town. We sit and talk and have a great time. Sometimes we actually eat there."

I am sure there was more to the conversation but somehow that is all I remember.

When I finished my project, I felt proud. "Look, I'm finished!" I told others. Then I put my hand on top of the miniature sled and it collapsed. The problem with glue is it simply doesn't work. That even seems to be true for the super strong glue I buy at the hardware store and use for household projects today. It doesn't seem to work any better than the kids' glue we used at camp and school.

Even after I finished my project, I hung out at the craft hut until the end of the craft period. When that end came, a boy only slightly younger than me approached Isabella.

"Hey, Thomas," Isabella told him cheerfully. I was taken by the way they looked into each other's eyes when they met. They walked away from the hut very close to each other. Then I left the craft hut to go back to the Shoshone hut.

My next activity was Games. I made my way to the clearing where this activity would take place. A conversation that one of the campers had with Chris drifted to the subject of dating. The conversation spread to a few of the other campers there. Chris then polled us to see if we wanted to play some kind of ball game or continue talking about dating and relationships. Almost all campers there chose the dating discussion. I did not vote for either option. One thing I remember clearly is one of the girls asked this hypothetical question: "What if the guy I am on a date with farts?"

"You can later tell him that you think it's gross. I wouldn't tell him during the date, but I would mention it later."

"If you're not going to be frank in the relationship, it's not going to work," one of the girls chimed in.

"That is an example of what not to do," Chris felt sure about what he was telling us here. "Girls, what positive things would you want a guy to do for you on a date?"

Another girl answered the question. "I like for the guy to hold the seat out for me to sit in when we are at a restaurant,"

One of the boys responded. "That's a nice thing for a guy to do. I would be glad to be nice to my date, but love is a two-way street. What nice things would my date do for me? Could a girl hold a seat out for a guy?"

Later, the conversation drifted to the subject of drugs and alcohol.

"Has anybody ever offered you booze at a party?" Chris was still talking to all of us.

"Yes," a girl answered, "but they respect your beliefs if you say 'no.'"

"That's the important thing."

Chris and the campers continued to make fascinating points. Chris later shared with us that he was impressed by the thought we were putting into the discussion. I could say that I was impressed too. Nonetheless, when time for the activity to end came, I was ready to move on.

When I was walking from the Games activity to Archery and crossing the bridge that spans the creek, I saw Stacy crossing the other way. "Hi, Tom. Where are you going?" Stacy had a sincere unforced smile.

"Archery."

"I'm going to Games."

"That's funny. I just left Games. I am having to go to the other end of the camp to get to Archery."

"Really?"

"Yeah. It's in a clearing."

"I will see you around, Tom."

This brief conversation ended there, and Stacy had been projecting warmth the whole time.

Shortly before it was time to go to the mess hall for dinner, Adam and Bobby approached me. "We would like to talk to you," Adam seemed to be content to do the speaking for both of them. I felt the same kind of dread that I feel whenever I am asked to go to the principal's office. I didn't get in much trouble at school, but I always felt nervous whenever I was called into that office or any other office.

Adam and Bobby led me to the front steps of our hut. The same Aztec who asked us about camping out was already there. He was holding something in his hand that looked like a badge.

"Hi, I'm Scott," the Aztec introduced himself. "You know that periodically we give out the PMA award and that 'PMA' stands for 'Positive Mental Attitude.' After talking to others, we have decided to give that award to you."

Scott handed me the badge.

The PMA Award was given out daily. Yesterday, Brandon Rhodes, the only African American camper in our hut, won it.

"Go ahead," Scott was puzzled by my apparent lack of enthusiasm. "Put it on."

I shyly and reluctantly did so.

"Now one reason we gave it to you is because when I went around asking who would like to go camping, you were enthusiastic about it while the others reacted negatively. Actually, we had to cancel the campout trip but that's beside the point."

I carefully placed the badge on the front of my shirt using the attached pin. I have always been wary of using pins to attach things to myself because I fear that I may stick myself. As I hung out with the other boys in front of our hut, I wondered if I really deserved the PMA award. I thought about times that I was not positive at home and at camp. I wondered if keeping the badge was the right thing to do. Finally, I caved into my modesty, "Do I really deserve this PMA?" Bobby assured me that I did.

After Archery I went back to the hut and stayed until time to go to dinner. When we were all lined up outside the mess hall, I saw Thomas and Isabella together. They were intently looking into each other's eyes with serious expressions on their faces and slowly walking while seeming oblivious to the world around them. They were obviously very involved with each other.

That night after dinner, all of the older campers gathered in the same clearing where I had done Archery a few hours earlier. It was Indian Night. We sat Indian style of course. We were introduced to a man named Marcus Littlebear.

Chapter Six

The man had a slightly darker tone to his skin than that of myself or the other White campers but not nearly as dark as that of the Black campers. He also did not appear to be an Asian American (and there were some of them among the camping population too).

"Hello. My name is Marcus Littlebear. I am a Native American living in the Yakama Nation Indian Reservation, and I work at a car dealership in Wapato. It is great to talk to all of you. There are a great many of us who dress, work, and live like everyday Americans. Yet I have not forgotten my Native American heritage.

"I would like to tell you a story. Our roots in this country go back about 10,000 years, farther back than the roots of anyone else in this country or this side of the world for that matter. My ancestors went across the Bering Strait which separates Alaska from the Soviet Union. Back then it was dry land and therefore easy to cross because this was during the Ice Age and more of the world's water was trapped in ice near the North and South Poles. Once we crossed that land bridge we kept moving until we lived in all parts of North and South America. A few of us even made our way to some of the Caribbean islands."

"From time to time we fought among ourselves, but for thousands of years we, for the most part, lived in peace. We lived in harmony with nature, treating it with deep respect and reverence. We only took from the natural world what we needed. We fished. We grew crops. We became experts at tracking people by simply looking at the ground. We produced beautiful pottery. We raised children."

"That all started to change in 1492 when Christopher Columbus came to this side of the world from a faraway land. There were Europeans who explored and settled the Americas before that year and a few people from other continents too. But the really lasting contact started around the 16th Century. As more of them came and settled, the White man demanded more and more of our land. Wars broke out between us and the White man. This country's government repeatedly broke its word to us forcing us to leave land we had been on for thousands of years and resettle somewhere else only to be asked again to move from that land. We fought to defend ourselves bravely, but it was hopeless. We had bows and arrows, but the White man had guns and cannons. Countless members of our tribes were killed. Many more died from diseases brought from Europe by the White man. Our once thriving Native American population dwindled to almost none compared to the White man or the Black man or the other peoples who came to this land later. There are Indian reservations in this country, but they are dirt poor. For the most part we live on land that the White man doesn't want. We are dominant in the Northwest Territory of Canada and in Greenland but those are among the coldest, most desolate places in North America. Life is also hard in the reservations sprinkled throughout the United States. Yet for thousands of years and even up to this day, we have proudly preserved our customs, culture, and identity."

I was spellbound by the rhythm, passion, and depth of Marcus's story. I thought of the stories I had been taught in school about our country's military and its accomplishments. But I could not condone the countless military actions I had heard and read about against Native Americans who were not bothering us. Several years after I finished school, I read a book which suggested that most of the Indians died from diseases brought over by the European settlers, diseases the Natives had no defense against. This certainly wasn't the Europeans' fault. Nonetheless many Native Americans were killed and the whole story saddens me to this day.

The question-and-answer session began. Marcus fielded questions asked by campers and even a few camp staff members. I can't say I remember all of the questions but many of the questions and answers were as follows.

"Do you hunt and fish?"

"To me, hunting is finding the appropriate aisle for the kind of food I want to buy at the supermarket. Some of us go out into the woods hunting and do fishing at the stream but mostly for recreation just like it is for most other Americans. One final point on that question is we always eat what we hunt and fish. We do not want any animal to give its life for nothing."

"Have you ever worn war paint?"

"On occasion, I will wear traditional tribal clothes including war paint at special ceremonies but no. I do not wear war paint to my day job, around the house, or at any time other than the occasional ceremonies I mentioned. As I mentioned earlier, the way I dress is indistinguishable from how other kinds of Americans dress."

"I have heard that Indians have great tracking skills. Do you?"

"Although tracking is not nearly as useful to us today as it was to our ancestors, my father did teach me quite a bit about how to track wildlife and people in a natural setting."

"Have you ever faced prejudice?"

"When I was a child, it was hard for my father to find work off the reservation if they knew he lived on a reservation. Acceptance of Native Americans is much better now than it was back then. Things are not perfect now. Some of the cartoons I have seen of Native Americans on sports team logos are not very flattering. But again, Native Americans have made a lot of progress towards equality just like Blacks and Mexicans have."

"Do you believe in God?"

"If you are asking what traditional Native American religion is like, the best way I can explain it is that it is nature centered and full of legends. I go to a Christian church, but I still see the natural world as sacred."

"Do you have any pets?"

"I have a dog."

"If Indians think the natural world is so sacred, why do Indians hunt?"

"My father used to take me hunting. We would always eat the animals we hunted and killed. Indians have hunted and fished throughout history. The difference is that we took from the natural world only what we needed."

"Do you have a family?"

"My wife and daughters were not able to make it here."

It was not long until Marcus politely wrapped up the question-and-answer session and mentioned something about needing to get home. I was fine with that.

Later that night after we waited patiently for it, a bonfire was lit in the field in front of us. A camp staff member led us in a rally. He addressed each hut individually as though each hut was a Native American tribe. Our huts were named after Native American tribes anyway.

"There is a special medicine that every tribe here needs to have in case one of us gets ill. To find this medicine we must all go into the forest which is a very dangerous place. We must all be brave. Each tribe here needs to choose a leader. That leader must be very brave and very wise. Begin talking among yourselves who you want to be your leader."

The people in our hut looked at each other. We had been tasked with choosing a leader among ourselves. Adam told us that it could not be him or Bobby since they wanted us to choose someone who was not a counselor. I was impressed with the modesty of the campers in my group because all I heard were several instances of campers telling fellow campers "You would be a good leader," and that camper who would say "Actually I wouldn't." If a camper in our group had told us "I should be the leader," I would have been okay with him being conceited enough to think that as long as he was humble enough to accept that he did not have the final exclusive word on who the leader would be.

Before long, Logan was chosen to be our leader for this event.

"Have you chosen a leader?" the camp staff member apparently needed an answer.

Every camper in every hut then loudly answered "Yes" in unison.

"All leaders come forward."

Logan stepped forward in front of us but still close to our group.

"Come up to me."

Logan did so.

Logan and the campers that the other huts had apparently chosen as leaders were soon gathered in front of the staffer and the bonfire.

"You have all chosen well," the staffer praised us.

He then turned to the hut leaders, and it looked a little bit like he was pretending to pray for them. "May the spirits be with all of you," he told them.

The leaders returned to their groups. Soon we all began walking towards the path that went from the clearing back to the cabins. The leaders walked in front of their groups of course. As I walked, I wondered what we would do next. Would there be another rally or perhaps some kind of game? When we reached our hut, it became clear that the night of events was over. The search for medicine in the forest was apparently just a fun way to describe being dismissed from Indian Night. Later that week, there would be an actual hunt for something.

Chapter Seven

Tuesday, July 2, 1985

Shortly after we had returned to the cabin from breakfast, it was time to go to the Rotunda for an assembly. The Rotunda had a roof but was open air. The roof was made of wood and the rest of the structure was stone and concrete. Our hut settled into an area of the Rotunda for seating which consists of no chairs. It is merely large steps, large enough to sit comfortably. Joey (a.k.a. Cyndi Lauper) was to my right. Other guys from the Shoshone hut were in the seats surrounding me.

"Tom," I heard from above. I looked back and up for the source of the voice. It was Stacy who, by the way, was very pretty. "Do you want to come sit up here?" she was patting an empty space next to her with her hand. The odd thing is that so many of the adjectives to describe how I felt at this moment all start with the letter 'e': excited, ecstatic, exhilarated, and euphoric. To say I was flattered out of my mind would be a vast understatement.

After a lightly spoken "excuse me" to Cyndi Lauper, I began making my way to that seat two steps higher, the highest level available. I took my seat with Stacy to my right. Once I was seated Stacy and I briefly looked at each other smiling ear to ear. One of the Aztecs was speaking to us. The program was religious in nature. That is all I noticed about it. I couldn't pay attention to the speaker. All I could think about was that I was sitting next to Stacy. The reason she invited me to sit by her couldn't have been because she felt sorry for me. I appeared perfectly content to sit with the guys in my hut. It was more likely because she was attracted to me. *Unreal!*

I put my arm on Stacy's back. "Huh?" she responded cheerfully when I did this. Here I lucked out. She thought I was merely trying to get her attention. I realized that Stacy was not ready for me to put my arm around her and without her thinking I was trying to do that. Had she thought I was trying to make this sexual advance, Stacy would have been uncomfortable. After Stacy's extremely brief response, I simply offered a polite, "Good to see you," and quickly waved my hand. The top level of the Rotunda was not very high up; just about ten feet. But even if I had been sitting in the highest row of the Kingdome, it would not have matched how high I felt then.

The assembly had to eventually end, and it did. When Stacy and I walked down and away from the Rotunda and as we were parting ways, I managed to speak to her despite being stunned in the best possible way, "I hope to see you around again soon."

A few seconds later, Cyndi Lauper caught up to me and walked beside me as we both made our way back to the Shoshone hut. "That was Stacy," he informed me although I already knew her name.

"I know," I answered in an almost dreamy state.

"You're really lucky," he seemed to be happy for me.

Later that day right after we had all returned from lunch, I noticed that Adam was looking around in his room. This was a very small room in the hut where he slept and kept his personal items. Bobby had a similar room. Adam was acting as though he had misplaced something valuable and was looking for it. A moment later, I noticed Adam leave the hut and go to the director's hut. When he came back, he had news for us. "I am missing my radio and the director wants the camp to assemble at the amphitheater." The amphitheater was a rarely used outdoor facility with stadium style seating and a space for performances.

We dutifully walked to the amphitheater. Adam's radio was missing which presented the possibility that it was stolen. This was serious business. The thought of sitting by Stacy again was driven far from my mind. It took several minutes for all of the campers to get settled in and seated. Finally, Benjamin Heimer got in front of the crowd and began speaking.

"It has come to my attention that Adam Craig's radio is missing. I don't know how this happened. I don't know if it was stolen but even if it was, whoever stole it is being given the chance to give it back to Adam and he will not say anything. Camp activities are suspended until Adam has his radio again. This may seem unfair, but we are hoping that the peer pressure will encourage you to help get Adam's radio back to him. You are welcome to search all of your belongings or search anywhere you think it might be. It is a yellow and black head set similar to a Walkman but it's not a Walkman. You may all return to your cabins."

After we got back to the hut, we were looking under beds and under piles of clothes for the radio. I checked my suitcase even though I did not remember picking it up. Other campers in our hut did the same. While I was helping Ray look under one nearby bed he protested, "This is not just unfair. It's a rip-off! My parents paid a lot of money so that I can do these activities and now I can't do them because Adam can't keep up with his radio."

I really didn't know what to say. He had a point. There is one good thing that had come out of this activity suspension and I will give credit to camp management for this. After about thirty minutes, all of our cots and surrounding personal space was much neater and more orderly. Perhaps campers had tidied up and organized their spaces as a part of searching for the radio. Maybe they were trying to impress the camp staff into resuming activities. Later Logan was sweeping the floor. When asked, he explained that Bobby had given him the broom upon request. Eventually the floor was completely swept, and everyone had their belongings well organized. The hut looked great.

"Well done, guys," Bobby praised us after his inspection. "We may even get Honor Hut." This comment surprised me and most of the other campers. Honor Hut is an award given to the "best" hut at the end of the week. It garnered very little enthusiasm even among the leaders. "But Adam's radio still has not been found."

"What if Adam drops the charges?" Paul was trying to think of a quick way the crisis could end.

"They won't let him."

A few minutes later, an adult camp staffer came by and talked to Bobby. We knew something had changed. A moment later Bobby told us there would be another meeting at the amphitheater. We all dutifully walked back to that venue. We did not know what would happen. One camper, while we were walking to the amphitheater, had even speculated that they may send us all home.

This time people settled into their seats and areas more quickly and Benjamin Heimer took less time until he began addressing us. "I told you earlier that all activities were on hold until Adam's radio was found," he began. "Now all camp activities will resume and take place at their regular time. The reason for this is because radios are not supposed to be here in the first place. So, if you lose your radio, don't come crying to us. You will keep things like that here at your own risk." I did remember seeing written material sent to my home from the camp in which radios were on a "please do not bring" list.

Things went back to normal rather quickly. When I got back to the cabin, it was still a few minutes until time to go to my next activity which was Games. One thing occurred to me which disgusted me. I had missed the Craft activity where I would have seen that awesome girl who asked me to sit by her. I did catch up with her later. When I was coming back from the Games activity, Stacy was walking in the opposite direction. We met up.

"Hi, Stacy," I was hoping to start a conversation with her, and I did.

"Hi, Tom."

There was one thing I wanted to learn from her, and I thought it was essential for our relationship.

"What's your last name?"

"Sapp."

"You mean 'Sap' as in the stuff that comes out of a tree?"

"No. S-A-P-P."

"Oh."

Stacy moved on as though she was in a hurry. She probably was. A moment later as I was walking to my hut, I saw Stacy's friend Isabella. She was with Thomas holding his hand. I was becoming more and more convinced that they were not only a couple but a close couple.

That night after dinner, one of the Aztecs came by our hut. We all gathered near him to hear what he had to say. "Tonight, there will be a special activity. It's a treasure hunt. The treasure is a golden horseshoe. The goal is for your hut to find this treasure before any other hut does. You will have clues. One clue will lead to another clue until a clue leads you to the actual horseshoe. Here is your first clue: go to Gregory Hall." Gregory Hall was a building near the director's hut and also resembled the director's hut at least from the outside but was somewhat bigger than the director's hut. In past camp sessions I had been to, we had been shown movies in there and watched demonstrations of amazing tricks there. What I remember most vividly, and it seems odd that I remember this, is a time when a wasp invaded the hall and one of the adult camp staffers sprayed it with bug killing spray and the wasp immediately dropped to the floor and died.

"Here are the rules," the Aztec continued. "If you get to Gregory Hall and it is empty, any other hut that arrives while you are there has to stay outside and be fifty feet from the building. If on the other hand another hut is in there when you arrive, it is you who must stay fifty feet away from that building. The same goes for all the other facilities the clues guide you to. When you find the horseshoe, bring it to the director's hut. You may leave your hut at eight o'clock. One of us will go around the camp playing the tune 'First Call' on a bugle when that time comes. Good luck."

Chapter Eight

We milled around the hut until it was time to go on the treasure hunt. It seemed like a long wait but eventually we heard the bugle outside. The tune sounded familiar. It took me a minute, but I remembered that it is the tune that they play at the Kentucky Derby. We made our way to the door of our hut in a slow, orderly fashion. When we were all out the door of the cabin, we bolted and ran towards Gregory Hall. We scurried around the inside of the building for clues. The place seemed normal. The audience chairs were neatly in place.

I was with Mark and Paul when we found something carved into the wooden wall. Crudely carved in letters no more than an inch high was "Wininger." That was the name of the gym at camp. "Over here," Mark was excited by his discovery. "This says 'Wininger!'"

"The prize is at the gym," Paul added.

"Either that or the next clue is," Logan speculated. By this time several other teammates had gathered with us by the carving.

In a matter of seconds, we were out the door and headed towards Wininger Gym. We were lightly running towards the bridge which had to be crossed to get to the gym. The night air was fresh and gentle. I felt the strong cohesion of our group as we ran together towards that next clue. I felt as though I were part of a primitive band of humans hunting a large animal and needing to work together and follow a leader. The night sky was surprisingly bright. It was a full moon that night and this moon was visible when we were in the clearing made by the river the bridge went across. Even though the hour was late, the night had just begun because sunset was so late at that time of the year in Washington state.

We entered the gym. As was the case with Gregory Hall, there seemed to be nothing out of the ordinary. Except the gym lights were on. Apparently, the camp staff left the lights on for us anticipating that we would go to Wininger Gym for clues. There was nothing on the green carpeted gym floor but that didn't mean that there were no clues on the stage. One member of our band pointed towards the stage and suggested we go there.

There was this riddle written on a portable chalkboard on the stage:

"I hang over something
that takes the shape of its container.
I am made of something
that was once alive."

"What does it mean?" Paul took the initiative.

"It's supposed to be hard to figure out what it means," was Mark's non-answer. "It's a riddle."

I began to help the group out by thinking. Then it hit me. It made me glad I studied hard and did well in physical science class when I was in the ninth grade. I remembered liquid having a precise description in science. Liquid takes the shape of its container. That was the very definition of a liquid. It was something I was aware of almost all my life but had never seen it verbally described.

"It's water!" I exclaimed. "Water takes the shape of its container. It has to be talking about Jasmine's Creek."

"You're right," Cyndi Lauper answered and then asked a question. "But what hangs over Jasmine's creek?"

"Tree branches?" Hank speculated.

I thought of the bridge, but that does not really hang over the water. It goes straight across it. Thinking how pretty the view of the water was when crossing the bridge led me to think about the beautiful view of the water from the deck where we sometimes had meetings and devotionals. Then I had another brainstorm. A deck is made of wood which was once a part of living things.

"It's the deck over Jasmine's Creek!" Taylor beat me to it.

We all took off for that deck. When we got there, the place looked very different at night. We could barely see the wooden railing. We heard the water rushing below. There were very small waterfalls there. I wondered how they expected us to be able to see any clue in the darkness.

"Does anyone have a flashlight?" I was surprised that we had gotten this far without one.

Hank produced one and turned it on. He aimed it at the floor of the deck first. We did not see anything but a small twig on the floor even after he thoroughly searched the floor with his flashlight.

"Maybe we got the location wrong," Mark speculated.

"Where do you think it is?" Taylor did not relish the thought of having to search another place.

"I don't know."

"Maybe there is a note somewhere here."

Hank slowly covered the perimeter of the railing with his flashlight. While the rest of us were speculating on where the next clue was and other possible meanings of the riddle, we were interrupted.

"I found something!" Soon more of us were looking at what Hank found. He was looking at an odd series of numbers and dashes chalked onto the deck floor.

"That's Morse code," Taylor seemed proud to be able to recognize it. "My dad learned it in the Navy and taught it to me."

"Can you read that?" Mark knew that recognizing a language and being able to read it were two different things.

"Let's see. The first letter is 'M'. The second letter, well, I'm trying to figure out if this dot is separate from the first three dots. If it is, then the next two letters are 'E' and 'S.' The letter after 'S' is also 'S.'" It didn't take him long to figure out that the Morse message read "mess hall." We all took off for the mess hall. Again, we had to cross the bridge over the creek. The lights to the mess hall had been turned on. Some of the tables had white plates on them. We looked on the tables and on the floor for something that might be a clue. Nothing. The walls and windows were also bare of any clue.

"How about the kitchen?" Hank suggested. We went to the door from the dining room into the kitchen. There was a cart blocking the door suggesting that we were not supposed to go in the kitchen and the clue was not in there.

"Are you sure this is the right place? Hank was beginning to feel like we had misunderstood the clue.

"The message was clear," Taylor insisted.

I walked around the tables feeling impatience and frustration. Some of us even tried lifting the plates and looking under them.

"May I have your attention?" Logan was trying to be a leader.

Silence.

"Perhaps we should admit defeat here. We had a good run, but we apparently can't find the next clue at what is unquestionably the location of that clue. We had might as well go back to our hut and wait for the assembly at the end of this contest. We can find out who won then. On the other hand, maybe we will find one of the other huts running towards a clue, possibly the next clue after this one, and we can follow them."

We began slowly reluctantly leaving the building. "Wait a minute," I had noticed something and spoke in a slightly raised voice to call everybody's attention to it. "See the plates? It looks like they are arranged in the shape of an arrow."

"But where is it pointing to?" Hank still needed to know.

"There are so many things in that direction it could be almost anything," Paul noted. Fervent discussion continued among us about the newly discovered clue. Again, we seemed to be back to square one. Finally, Ray made a comment that was borderline funny. "The only purpose this arrow is serving for me is to remind me that I have archery tomorrow."

"That's it!" Logan suddenly understood. "This arrow isn't pointing anywhere. It's an arrow because the next clue is in the place where arrows are used, the archery range."

We were unsure of this interpretation of the clue. Nonetheless we agreed to head towards the archery range. It was farther away than the other clues we had raced towards. We had to not only cross the bridge back to the area where the residential huts were but also walk through that area to a path which led away from the huts and towards a clearing. We didn't even run towards the archery area. It was so far away that running towards it would take up more of our energy that we wanted.

As we walked down that path and through the night air, I was beginning to wonder how many clues there was. Hopefully this would be last one and it would be explicit instructions as to where the golden horseshoe was. They didn't say how many clues would only lead to another clue so there could be a lot more of them. Maybe another five more. Maybe six. If so, we were in for a long night. I had a feeling, though, this was the last one.

There were trees on either side of us as we walked on the path until we finally reached the clearing. We made our way to the archery targets. I noticed that only one of them had an arrow in it. I made it to the arrow first. It held a message on a small piece of paper to the target. We needed Hank's flashlight to see what was on the piece of paper. A relief came over all of us when we found that the piece of paper did not have an obscure riddle or coded message on it. It had a map. The map would lead us to the golden horseshoe; this we knew because a horseshoe was drawn on the map and was inside a square labeled "craft hut." The map as a whole was an extremely crude layout of Camp Sunbeam. Some of us actually vocally cheered. Personally, for me, in addition to being happy to know where the prize was, the mention of the craft hut brought a chilling sensation of excitement and happiness to me because it reminded me of Stacy Sapp, the cute girl who invited me to sit by her earlier today. Stacy was in the craft activity session with me.

This time we were not worried about fatigue or the long distance, so we ran to the craft hut. We certainly did not want another hut to beat us to it. After we came out of the other end of the path and into the hut area, I looked around to see if other groups were running towards the prize too. I did not see any.

We were a little bit more careful and not as fast when we crossed the bridge. After we had crossed the bridge and passed the gym we were in less forested area where craft hut was. "There it is," Logan was pointing straight ahead. "That's the craft hut." Ahead was the dark outline of a very small building. It was impossible for me to identify as the craft hut at night, but Logan was convinced that this was the hut. When we got to the craft hut, Logan immediately canvassed the structure and nearby tables with his flashlight. There in plain view was the golden horseshoe hanging from a nail on the wall. We all cheered of course.

"Tom, will you do the honors and pick up the horseshoe and take it to the director's hut. We will follow." I felt honored. Furthermore, the other campers made it a point to follow me from behind as though I were some kind of leader. I thought about that cute girl I sat with earlier today. If she saw me carrying the horseshoe, she would be impressed even though it was a team effort, and she knew it. Just three days into camp and already things were going great. My hut had won the treasure hunt and I had won a pretty girl's heart.

When we go to the director's hut, I triumphantly opened the door and announced, "We got it!"

Benjamin Heimer was in front of us. "Well done. Your hut has won fourth place."

What!?

We didn't have to say "what" out loud. It was in our faces and our silence. Finally, one of us spoke up. "But we have the treasure right here," Cyndi Lauper protested.

"The Teninos' found it first. My assistant Rick was watching the craft hut the whole time. When they took the horseshoe, he replaced it with another one. He did this each time a hut found the treasure."

Naturally there was grumbling among our troops.

"Don't feel bad. You guys did great. Those clues were hard to understand. All this means is that all of our campers are smart," Heimer's efforts to console us were not successful. "Now the award ceremony is at the gym. It will be in about twenty minutes. Be sure to be there. In fact, I encourage you to go ahead and go now so your group can get good seats."

There was nothing we could do. We could not protest because there was no reason to think the results of the contest were wrong. We reluctantly filed out and began walking slowly towards Wininger Gym.

The awards ceremony did not have a lot of suspense to it. We knew what place we finished in. We even knew who won first prize. Here is what we did find out. The award for first prize was two days of free Oasis. We also found out who won second prize which was one day of free Oasis and the third-place winners got a piece of candy for each camper. When it was our turn, our prize was announced. "Fourth prize goes to the Shoshone hut. They will receive an all-expenses paid trip to beautiful, exciting, exotic, thrill-packed, star-studded Happy, Washington."

Happy, Washington was (and still is) a town very close to the Oregon state line and close to Portland. The description they gave of Happy is sarcastic. It was a very small town with very little tourism. That is the way it was back then. Now it is more or less a suburb of Portland and is growing fast.

The director thanked us all for coming to the awards assembly and we went back to our huts. Please do not misunderstand me. I was just as bummed out about not winning the contest when we thought we had won it as anyone else in our hut was. But on the way back to our cabin, I was thinking about how much fun I had on the chase. My mind was also too busy to sulk because I was trying to come up with ways to meet up with Stacy again. The craft activity which I was taking with Stacy was over. We would both be doing something else then. Two possibilities: (1) Hope that she is in one of the new activities I start tomorrow or (2) find her when she lines up for breakfast or some other meal tomorrow.

After all Stacy still has to eat.

61

Chapter Nine

Wednesday, July 3, 1985

This morning I knew exactly what I wanted to do. I wanted to find Stacy and have a conversation with her. I hoped to find her lined up for breakfast before they opened the doors to the mess hall. Our group left the hut and went to the mess hall. When we got there, we were behind some of the younger campers. Behind us another group of campers came up. I couldn't believe my good luck. It was a group of girls about Stacy's age which meant that Stacy might be among them. After just a few seconds of looking, I found Stacy herself in the group. I made my way over to her. I wanted to get to her and visit with her as long as possible before the mess hall doors were opened, and I had to go in with the rest of my own group.

"Good morning, Stacy," I felt more confident than ever as I talked to her.

"Oh, hey there," Stacy returned the greeting.

"Is this your first time to come to Camp Sunbeam?"

"Not even close. I have been coming here for about five or six years. Is this your first time here?"

"No. This is my third year to come here. I was here last year and in 1983. Where do you go to school?"

"This fall I will start at Tyler County High School."

"Are you excited about it?"

"Sure. High school is big and scary, but I know it can be exciting. It's just a school."

"What subjects are you going to take?"

"I don't know yet."

"What is your family like? Do you have any brothers or sisters?"

"I have an older sister named Camille."

I told her about my family and my school and that I was very happy there. I even told her about our pets including the cat I thought of as my own.

"Oh, I love cats," Stacy's face lit up upon mentioning cats. "But we don't have cats, just dogs. Actually, just one dog. My dad likes to go hunting with the dog. It's a nice outing away from his job. He works as a loan officer at the Bank of Lakota." I was about to ask Stacy what her father's occupation was, and I am glad she saved me the trouble.

The girls around us started moving. I realized that they were headed towards the door of the mess hall which had been opened. This meant that my group was headed into the hall, and I needed to rejoin them.

"I gotta go," I was thankful that the conversation, though short, lasted as long as it did.

"Ok."

In the mess hall after most people had finished breakfast, "May I have your attention?" boomed loudly enough to get most people's attention. The voice came from a young man who may have been one of the Aztecs. He went on to give us a lecture. Actually, I don't know whether to call it a lecture. It was more like a sermon in an informal devotional.

The sermon was about standing for and fighting hard for what you believe. One line in his lecture stood out to me. "Do you remember from *The Karate Kid* when Mr. Miyagi taught Daniel to always walk on one side of the road or the other side, never in the middle?" After this speech, Benjamin Heimer made a few announcements. One of the announcements was that there would be a big dance on the last night of camp.

On the way back from breakfast, I witnessed something that both ered me. I wish to this day that I had done something about it. Ryan was walking with a camper I hadn't seen before. "I am on my school's football team and in practice they teach you how to hit a player on the other team with your whole body."

"Really?" the other camper sounded impressed.

"Yeah. You have to hit at just the right spot. Let me show you."

Ryan then started running in a beeline towards Ray who happened to be walking toward him and was less than twenty feet away. Ryan struck Ray with his shoulder knocking him down.

"I have had enough of that shit!" Ray angrily swept pebbles on the ground in Ryan's direction.

Even worse is that the fact that Ray's "I have had enough" implied that Ryan had been doing things like this to him for a while.

A moment later, I saw Thomas and Isabella together again walking and looking into each other's eyes. This reinforced my impression that they must really like each other.

"Who is going to be your date to the dance?" I overheard one of the campers say when we were back in our hut.

"I don't know. Maybe Becky," was the answer he got. Several other campers made comments about who they would like to ask to be their date to the dance. This dance had been announced during breakfast, but I didn't think much of it at the time. I just thought it would be some big party. But if this was an event one could take a date to, I knew exactly who I wanted to ask.

A few seconds later, the subject changed dramatically. Scott, one of the Aztecs, paid us a visit and asked us if we wanted to go caving. We would enter and explore a cave at the side of a mountain (probably the mountain I saw when I first arrived at camp). I was one of six volunteers to go caving. The others were Hank, Juan, Pete, Mark, and Brandon. "You are all going to want to shower off afterward," Scott was giving us a heads-up. We nonetheless followed him out the door of the cabin. I had heard exciting stories about people finding beautiful and fascinating things in caves. I had seen a *Smurfs* cartoon about a leprechaun finding a huge treasure inside a cave. Another *Smurfs* cartoon featured a cave with bountiful food behind a wall of ice during a drought. I was under no illusions about actually finding treasure in the cave we were going to, but cave exploration was an exciting idea for me.

We walked until we arrived at a crude bus with the camp's name on it. There were only seven of us, so we really did not need the whole bus, but that was probably all they had. We all took seats toward the front of the bus. The bus first got on the paved road that my mother took to bring me to camp. It was the only road leading to and from Camp Sunbeam. In fact, it was called Sunbeam Road. After about five minutes, we turned off onto a dirt road. This could have been interpreted as an ominous sign. Any activity that we had to go onto a dirt road to get to must be treacherous. Then again that may just be a stereotypical assumption among all city kids and suburban kids. The dirt road began to wind up the mountain and the road became more challenging. It was narrower and rockier. We were close enough to the edge of the road that my primal fear of heights began to kick in. Just as this was happening though, the bus stopped.

It turned out that we had stopped not because we had arrived at the cave but because it was as far as we could safely travel in the vehicle. After walking about half of a kilometer we got to a relatively flat plain on the side of the mountain. Embedded in the side of a ridge was a crude fissure. I knew this was the cave we would explore.

Scott told us all to stop. It was apparently so he could give us instructions. "I will go in first of course. We will all now get in a single file line. When we are in the cave, do not ever be more than four feet behind the person in front of you in line. If you feel safer, you can put your hands on the back of the person in front of you in line. Those of you who brought your flashlights, that was a good idea. There are some parts of the cave where you will need both hands to get through. In those cases, you will need to find some other way to carry your flashlight." I began to wonder if he thought we needed to be wearing hard hats with flashlights mounted on them like miners wear.

We got in a single file line. We followed Scott into the cave. I felt cool, breezy air as soon as I entered the cave. Summers in the states of Washington and Oregon are mild, something I have been thankful for all my life. Nonetheless, I appreciated that the air inside the cave was cooler than the summer air outside it.

The ceiling of the cave was high. The ground was flat except for a few large stalagmites which were easy to walk around. There was just enough daylight pouring through the cave entrance so we could see the ceiling. Many stalactites, big and small, protruded from the ceiling. There were no jewels in the cave but some of the stalactites and some other parts of the ceiling were white and chalky in appearance and made the place brighter. Many campers shone their flashlights at the ceiling. It was a beautiful and exciting place.

"This way," Scott was standing near what appeared to be the end of the cave. We followed and the cave seemed to swallow him up. I was wondering how Scott and the campers in front of me could walk through the solid rock at the end of the cave. I was horrified to learn how. It was because they were actually entering a very small crevice at the end of the cave. Even worse, the only explanation for why those who went forward disappeared from view was because this much smaller part of the cave went downward. The journey would be treacherous.

When it was my turn to go through the hole, which I had to duck to get into, I was not greeted by nice cool air. Instead, the air felt musty and an odor of what I could only guess was that of dead bats. The cave got smaller, so small that we had to crawl to move forward. Even worse, the ground was somewhat muddy.

"Hang in there, guys," Scott was trying to encourage us. "We are almost at the end of the downward part of the cave." After what I am sure seemed longer than it actually was, there was a turn in the direction of the cave. The cave bent to the left and we were no longer going down. Now we were going up. This part of the cave was just as cramped and since we were going up, it took additional effort. Thankfully, it was not as damp. Then we heard multiple high-pitched squeaking noises.

"Bats," Juan speculated. Another thought on the source of the noises entered my mind. I had seen movies in which moist underground places like these had about a hundred rats. The thought creeped me out. I never understood why cartoons portrayed rats and mice as cute, pleasant, even heroic characters. In fact, the biggest family entertainment company in the world has a mouse not only as its most famous character but also as its logo. "The Mouse" is synonymous with this company.

The screeching not only continued but got louder. "We may be about to pass them right now," I heard one of the campers announce. If he thought it was funny that we would soon encounter whatever creatures were making those noises, he was wrong. It was something I didn't even want to know. After we had gone just a little farther, I felt something on my left shoulder. After hearing all those high-pitched squeaks in the cave, I almost let out a shriek of my own. *I'm at camp. I must be brave.*

I turned my head very slowly afraid of what I would see on my shoulder. Then I felt it move off me followed by a buzzing sound. I presumed it was some kind of insect. With the distraction of the insect gone, I began to again feel the difficulty of climbing. My fingers had to grab the earth in front of me time after time, and this earth was not reliably dry. We got to a part of the cave where we could walk if we bent down. This part of the cave was also level at first and later there was a gentle downward slope.

"Spider web ahead," Scott presumably would at least partially clear it for himself and the rest of us after giving this warning and going through it himself. I might feel some loose spider webbing but what really concerned me is that since this was a spider web, I would have to assume that there may be a spider nearby. That spider could be poisonous. It could bite me, and I could die. I imagined that if that happened, my parents would be able to sue Camp Sunbeam for so much money that they would never have to work again. No amount of money, however, would deaden the sorrow of losing a child. I had seen a news segment on television about people who have severe arachnophobia. All of their reading material has to be checked by others to make sure there are no pictures of spiders. I did not and still do not have this phobia. But I knew that some spiders were poisonous, and I did not know which kinds of spiders were.

Just as I was thinking these thoughts, I felt something small contact and begin crawling on my back shoulder. My blood froze. I presumed it was the spider who made this web. I wanted to knock it off my body immediately. But if I tried that, the spider would probably panic and bite me. Maybe it was just better to let the spider crawl on me feeling unthreatened and jump off me. The dilemma of what to do ended when I heard laughter right behind me. It came from Juan who had been right behind me the whole way. The creature I felt on my back was his fingers.

"Ha, ha, ha, ha, ha, ha. You looked terrified"

"Cut it out!" my voice was raised because of my anger. I would later have to apologize to Juan for snapping at him, but I was in no mood to be scared by a practical joke. The incident would have probably attracted Scott's attention if he had not been busy clearing the way forward for us.

Finally, we got to an area where we could all stand up straight. It was much wider too. "May I have your attention," we gave Scott out attention. "I am standing in front of a crevasse that we will have to jump gently across. It is about two feet wide. I will jump first and then I will be there to make sure all of you jump safely across. If anything goes wrong, I will be there to grab you." This was not very reassuring. "Do not jump until I tell you to."

When looking around the spelunkers in front of me, I could see Scott hop across the crevasse. Hank, who was first in line after Scott, stood over the crevasse. We had to back up so he could get a little of a running start. "Jump," Hank began moving towards the big crack when Scott gave the word. With no visible signs of nervousness, Hank propelled his body upward and over the crevasse landing on the other side. Pete was next. He was also the one right in front of me in line. Pete took more time preparing himself than the rest of us did. He seemed to be making absolutely sure it was safe for him to proceed. I obliged and left plenty of space for him. I also whispered, "Good luck" but I am not sure he heard me. Pete made his jump safely.

Now it was my turn. I wanted to make sure I was able to see everything clearly including the ground on the other side, and the people on the other side who had to be out of the way. I had seen our cats at home time a jump. If they could judge distance, so could I. I got a short running head start and jumped across landing on the other side with Scott there to almost catch me.

Juan was next after me. "I think I'll step across," he was starting to put his foot far forward to try to put it on the other side of the gap.

"No, you won't," Scott took his job of protecting us seriously. Juan pulled his leg back and began backing up to hop across. His jump and Brandon's jump went without incident. One more camper had to get across, Mark. Mark backed up more than any of us had to get his running start. It appeared far more than necessary. He said "Geronimo" and started running. When he was over the crevasse, Mark held his arms out and said "Wheeeeee!" Mark obviously wanted to have fun jumping across. There was only one problem. Mark not only held out his arms but also opened the palms of his hands wide and therefore dropped the flashlight he was holding. The flashlight dropped and interfered with his jump. His right foot came down on the other side just a centimeter away from the crevasse. Then his other foot came down on the ground. Mark was safely across. His flashlight was not so lucky. Mark watched in dismay as it fell down the seemingly bottomless crevasse. Eventually neither the flashlight nor light from it was visible.

"I saved up for two months on allowance to buy that flashlight," Mark lamented.

"What is infinitely more important is that you are okay," Scott responded to put the situation in perspective for Mark. "For a second, I wasn't sure you were."

"Over here, guys," Scott had already walked over to an opening in the side of the cave wall. The hole was elevated about one and a half meters above the floor of the cave. Scott went in headfirst. We all followed in the order that we had been going in for the entire trek. The climb was the steepest climb so far, but Scott kept reassuring us that this was the last leg of the trip. I was looking forward to seeing daylight, eating a delicious lunch, shooting a rifle (Riflery was on my schedule later in the day), breathing fresh air, and talking to Stacy. I was thinking that I needed to go ahead and ask Stacy to the dance party. Stacy was pretty and was therefore likely to be snatched up by some other guy. She seemed to like me, but I wasn't taking any chances.

While we were all crawling upward in what did not seem much less cramped than an air conditioning duct, I saw something that gave me hope that we were finally nearing the end of our journey. There was a branch from ten to twenty centimeters long with a few leaves on it. About a minute later, I noticed a hint of daylight in the cave. *Hooray!*

Motivated by the proximity of the metaphorical and literal light at the end of the tunnel, we all crawled onward and upward. For the first time, I noticed soreness on one of my shoulders. We relied on outward rock protrusions along the cave to climb. I felt almost like we were climbing a mountain. We passed more vegetation. This time it was part of a tree trunk and was roughly ten centimeters thick. It was probably part of the roots of one of those Douglas Fir or Western Hemlock trees. It was partly embedded in the earth on the side of the cave. A little bit higher up, there was a gap between it and the stone cave wall right below where it disappeared into the earth above. I moved past this section of tree just like I moved past the tiny tree branch earlier.

Then I saw the most beautiful sight since entering the cave. I saw the cave opening at the end and blue sky. Scott reached it and appeared to have his hand on the rim of the opening and his head above it. I could also feel the fresh air.

"I'm stuck," I recognized Mark's voice. When I looked down to see what Mark was talking about, I saw that he was almost but not quite past the tree root gap. "My foot is stuck," he whined. Upon closer inspection, I was dismayed to see that he was right. His foot was trapped in the opening between the tree root and the earth that formed the side of the cave.

"Is there something wrong?" Scott was responding to hearing Mark.

"Mark's foot is stuck in something," Brandon informed Scott.

"Help Mark," Scott's instructions were not just for Brandon but to any of us who could help out in freeing Mark. Still Brandon was closest, so he tried to pull Mark out by putting his hand in Mark's hand and pulling. He couldn't budge Mark.

"It didn't work," Mark continued to sound pessimistic not only in what he was saying but in his tone of voice. "I'm going to be stuck here for the rest of my life."

"We'll get you out," was the encouragement that Juan offered. Then he offered actual assistance. "Brandon, if you pull his right hand, I will pull his left hand. Maybe with the strength of both of us, we can get him out." So, Brandon climbed higher to be level with Juan. Then they began pulling both his hands at the same time.

"Owwww!" Mark cried out in pain. Apparently, not only was this not working, but the effort was also pulling him in a way that was painful to him. We did not want to injure him. I had heard of cases in which people administering first aid were advised not to move an unconscious injury victim because doing so might break the victim's neck. Of course, in this case it was not Mark's neck that was in danger. It was breaking a bone in his foot or spraining his ankle that we had to be careful to avoid. Then again, one of those injuries might have already taken place.

Chapter Ten

What caused me anxiety about Mark's situation is that I did not know how long it would last. I wanted to help, but I was a little bit too far up the cave. It would have been awkward and impractical for me to climb back down to Mark while Juan and Brandon got out of the way. All I could do was offer a suggestion. "Why don't you try moving his foot out of that snag?"

"I'll try that," Brandon volunteered. Brandon began wiggling his foot around. He firmly moved it in one direction. In fact, he tried to force Mark's foot in several directions, but it seemed that each time he did this he would free the foot from one part of the trap, but it would get stuck in another part of the trap.

"How's it coming down there?" Scott was checking in on Mark and those of us trying to help him.

"Will you guys bring me some food?"

"What are you talking about?" the request did not make sense to Scott at first.

"When you guys leave, will at least one of you come back and bring food. I am going to be stuck here for a long time. In fact, you may have to come with three meals for several days. Nothing that any of you are doing is working."

"Don't be so negative, Mark. We will figure out something."

"Tell my baby brother he can have everything in my room since I will never see home again and tell our Siberian husky at home I said goodbye."

Scott ignored the absurdity of what Mark was saying and offered another idea and it seemed to be the final idea. "Let's all pull to get Mark out. Hank, take my hand. Pete, grab Hank's hand. The rest of you join hands with the person ahead of you. Someone down there with Mark, I don't care who, grab his hand. Then we will all pull at the same time." Scott seemed to be hoping that the strength of all of us combined would be enough to get Mark's foot dislodged.

"I need you to take my hand," Juan instructed Mark while wondering if Mark would even have enough confidence to cooperate. Juan held out his hand while Mark's hand was trembling. For the longest time, this trembling was the only motion in his hand. Then, ever so slowly, Mark moved his hand towards Hank's. It took much longer than it should have, but Mark joined hands with Juan.

"Is everybody connected by hand?" Scott was clearly ready to get this over with.

"Yes," everyone below Scott seemed to say at once.

"Any 'no's?'"

After a few seconds of silence, Scott was able to presume that there were no campers who had not yet gotten the hand of their neighbor.

"All right," Scott continued. "On my count of three, we will all pull up. One, two, three!" I felt a sharp almost painful pull upward on my left arm from Pete. After about fifteen seconds, we stopped pulling. Mark was still stuck.

"We've got to try again," Scott was not quite ready to give up. We went through the same procedure again. No luck.

After we had twice failed to pull him out with our combined strength, Scott offered another idea. "There is some climbing cable in the bus. It is left over from when we used to do mountain climbing as an activity. First everyone besides Mark come on up out of the cave." We all slowly climbed out one at a time. Now we were standing over the cave. Part of me hated to leave Mark down there alone, but I suspected Scott had a reason for telling us to do that. Before I even finished that thought, Scott was already in the bus getting the cable he mentioned. It took him less than a minute to get the piece of climbing gear out of the vehicle and start heading back to us.

It was already clear what the Aztec had in mind. We would throw down this cable so Mark could grab it and allow us to pull on the rope and pull Mark up to safety. We still had to hope this would first free Mark's foot from the snag it was in. Scott threw the cable down the cave allowing it to unfold enough so it was as far down as Mark was. The cable was far enough down for Mark, but it was on the other side of the cave and therefore still out of Mark's reach.

"Mark, grab the cable," Scott instructed.

"I can't reach it," Mark responded.

"I have it far down enough."

"But it's on the other side."

Finally, Scott figured out what Mark was talking about. Scott moved around the mouth of the cave hoping to move the cable so that it was closer to Mark.

"I got it," Scott was visibly relieved to hear Mark say this.

Then upon Scott's instruction, he and all of the campers, including me, pulled on the cable away from the cave. There soon came a point when we could not pull anymore. I had a bad feeling about why. Scott approached the cave and seemed to talk to Mark but we couldn't make out exactly what he was saying. Then Scott walked towards us and conceded that Mark was still trapped.

"What do you guys want to do?" Scott must have been desperate if he was asking us for ideas. All Scott heard from us campers was either silence or indecipherable grumbling.

"All right," Scott's shoulders seemed to lower as he sighed. "I'll go find a phone somewhere and call emergency. You guys stay here with Mark." Scott began to walk away.

"Wait!"

The voice came from Hank. Scott walked back to the cave opening. Hank showed Scott a metal star about the size of the palm of his hand. It had five sharp points.

"What's that?" Scott was clearly puzzled.

"It's a ninja throwing star. I have a blue belt in karate. It is the fifth belt I have gotten." After Scott asked Hank what this had to do with the problem at hand, Hank continued.

"If I can throw this star accurately enough, I can strike the root or whatever it is that is holding Mark's foot in place and destroy it or at least weaken it enough so that he can get his foot loose."

"Okay," Scott reluctantly agreed, "but I would feel better if you had a black belt in karate."

Camp Sunbeam had a strict policy against possession of weapons. On the first day of camp, we were all given the opportunity to turn in any knives or weapons we had on hand or else face severe punishment if we were caught later in possession of any of them. Some campers did indeed have knives to hand over. Yes, I know there were rifles as well as bows and arrows in archery but those were used by campers only under close supervision of camp staff. In spite of this zero-tolerance weapons policy, I predicted that nothing would be said about Hank having this sharp-edged star if he succeeded in freeing Mark with it.

We all returned to the cave entrance. We all shone our flashlights down the cave towards Mark. It was so bright, he had to close his eyes. It was extremely important that the throw was accurate and that it hit only the root Mark's foot was stuck in and not his foot itself or any other part of Mark's body.

Hank took a deep, controlled breath and threw the Ninja star with as much strength and concentration as he could summon. The star hit the curved tree root and cut through most of it. This was enough for Mark to move his foot out of where it had been trapped for what I am sure seemed a very long time to him.

"How 'bout that, guys" Mark couldn't have been happier. "I'm free!" We left the climbing cable in place so that Mark would have extra help in getting out. Mark used this line as support from time to time, but generally did his own climbing.

Mark emerged from the cave and began standing on sunlit ground. Everyone else cheered. Mark then hugged Scott and all of the campers one at a time. "I love you guys. I don't ever want to be separated from you guys again. It is so great to be home."

Of course, we were not home. We were not even at Camp Sunbeam, our temporary home. But I understood why he said it. He was with the people who, for all practical purposes,   were family.

There was something none of us had noticed. Maybe it was because the cave was so dark. It may have also been because we were concentrating on moving, crawling, and climbing through the cave. At any rate, we had just become aware of the dirt and mud that was all over us. It was all over our clothes which we would not be able to wear again until they were washed if ever again at all. A trip to the shower station immediately upon getting back to camp was now a must.

We climbed back into the bus each one of us looking like something the cat declined to drag in. Then I had a horrible thought. What if Stacy saw me looking like this? Would she think I was so cute if I was covered in mud in various spots? On the other hand, Stacy was sweet and would understand that this was temporary, and I could easily wash up. If I explained, she might think it was brave of me to go in that cave. Of course, I wanted to get clean before I asked Stacy on a date, something I felt like I needed to do today. I wanted to get clean anyway.

The bus ride back to camp was quiet. Maybe it was because the seriousness of what had happened had dawned on us. Mark was lucky that one of us was able to get him out of that cave. Otherwise, we would have had to call civil emergency rescue workers such as those with the fire department to get him out, and I am not sure they would have been able to do it. By the end of the bus ride, we had lightened up a little bit and there was very limited chatter.

We each got off the bus feeling older and wiser. The first place we went after we got off the bus was to the Shoshone hut. We had to go there to get the bags we would use to store the clothes we would put on after showering. Scott escorted us there and then departed. When we entered the hut looking the way we did, Juan's only words for the others in the hut were, "Don't ask." We got our bags and clothes and went to the bathroom/shower hut.

When we were showering, there were conversations in which we shared our feelings about going through that cave. I mentioned how beautiful the cave was until we started going through that cubby hole about a minute after we entered the cave. Another one of us said it would have been okay if there had been no other creatures in the cave. The answer he got from the one whose voice I recognized as Brandon's was that the animals had to live somewhere.

"It's not my body I mind the mud being on," Pete was struggling to get clean just like we all were. "It's my hair." We eventually did all get clean and Scott joined us and began his shower just as we were finishing ours. I put on the clothes I had packed. I stood in front of the mirror to use the comb which I was glad that I also put in the bag. With my hair back in order, I took a good look at myself in the mirror. My appearance was decent, respectable, and ready for any chance encounter with Stacy. I felt clean and had on fresh new clothes. I felt like a new man.

When I got back to the hut, they were already getting ready to go to lunch. I did not have to worry about not having worked up an appetite. I made a mental note of the irony of going to a place we called the mess hall after being in that cave. All of us who had been in the cave were exempted from pig duties.

Chapter Eleven

On my way back from lunch, I saw Stacy alone. I knew I might not get another chance to talk to her alone, so I decided to ask her to the dance.

"Hi, Stacy."

"Hi, Tom."

We stopped close to each other, and I faced her. Yes, I know she has implied an interest in me. She did ask me to sit by her. I don't care. It's never easy asking a girl out.

"What activity did you just finish?" I decided that a very brief period of small talk would be the best way to prepare to ask her out.

" I just got done canoeing."

"Must have been fun."

"Yeah."

It was now or never. "Do you want to go to the dance with me?" I had to get the words out of my mouth quickly before I lost my courage.

I braced for a rejection. She responded to my question with a question of her own. "Are you talking about the dance party on the last day of camp?"

"Uh, yes. Will you go to it with me?" I hated that I had to ask again. It was hard enough the first time.

"Yes. I'll go with you."

I had to suppress the thrill of succeeding in getting a date with Stacy long enough to work out some details.

"Do you see that tree over there?" I pointed towards a Douglas Fir tree that was midway between the boys' side and the girls' side of the cabin area. I was afraid she might not know what tree I was talking about it. "Follow me and let me show you." I walked towards the tree, and she followed. I waited until we got to the tree before giving the instructions. "Meet me at this tree fifteen minutes before the dance and we will walk from there to the gym. I don't know exactly what time the dance is, only that it is at night. We'll find out later. But I will meet you fifteen minutes before the dance."

"Okay."

"I'll see you around," I started walking back to my hut.

I had closed the deal. While I was walking back to the cabin, I felt like I was walking on clouds instead of walking on the ground. My optimism was cautious. I didn't know if this relationship would last a few days or a few months. The latter would require the relationship to exist outside of camp. It didn't matter. I had just planned my first date ever. If I had not been worried about anybody seeing me, I would have jumped my way back to the hut instead of walking. Instead, the only visible sign that I was experiencing a moment of triumph was a bigger than usual smile.

When I walked into the hut, there were not a lot of people in there. However, Cyndi Lauper was in the hut talking to Taylor. "I am thinking about asking Amber to be my date," Taylor seemed to sense that Cyndi Lauper wanted Taylor to share that with him.

"Maybe you will see her at lunch. We are about to go there.," Cyndi Lauper reminded him.

It was not often that I got to brag about success with girls, so I joined the conversation. "I know who I'm taking."

"Who?" Cyndi Lauper was already excited for me and wanted to know.

"Stacy Sapp."

"That's really cool."

"Thank you."

A girl had asked me to sit by her at an assembly. That same girl had agreed to go on a date with me. To understand why all of this is so special to me, you have to know more about me when I was sixteen. I had enjoyed amazing achievements in academics. I was an honor student. I had won several best-in-class awards including one in Geometry in which I had a 99% grade average during one grading period. But for reasons I would not understand until years later, I struggled mightily in social interactions. You can imagine how difficult romance would be for someone like me.

At lunch I was in such a good mood because of Stacy that I didn't mind eating the healthy but terrible tasting food offered. I even got a wink from Stacy when I passed her table in the mess hall. *Awesome!*

My next activity was Pioneering. Like the caving excursion, this was a special one-time activity that I and the other participants agreed to join orally rather than by signing up for it. We went into the forest and an Aztec instructed us on tasks that pioneers would do when first settling in a new place. The Aztec, who identified himself as Carson, first told us to cut down very small thin trees with a small ax. He explained and demonstrated how to cut them down. Then he handed each of us an ax. Again, these were very small axes and therefore safe enough for older campers to use. Soon we were all chopping down trees that were no taller than we were. I soon realized why this was a one-time-only activity. All of the trees in this grove happened to be very small. Maybe there were other places like this near the camp but that seemed unlikely. On the other hand, maybe the camp staff planted all these little trees here so we could do this activity. At any rate, it seemed like it would take us no longer than a day or two to do whatever we were going to do.

"Now trim the branches off the tree," Carson ordered after we had all cut down trees. In most cases this was a simple matter of breaking the branches off with our hands. A few branches, however, were thick enough that we had to use our axes. Carson told us to put aside some of the smallest branches. "I will explain what to do with those later."

The next step was to lay the tree trunks on the ground to form a rectangle. We were told to call these pieces of wood logs and to lay them on top of each other with them interlocking at each corner. What we were beginning to form reminded me of the Lincoln Logs I played with earlier in my life. Eventually we ran out of logs and what we had built so far was not nearly high enough to be called a house.

Carson then pointed to the small loose twigs he had told us to put aside. "If we were real pioneers, we would have to have a way to heat our house and cook. These can be used for a fire."

Carson then turned his attention back to the house. "That will be all for today," he told us. "If any of you want to come back here at the same time tomorrow, we can finish the house." Personally, I wanted to go back to swimming which is what I did during this time slot the day before. Pioneering was interesting enough, but swimming would be far more refreshing than walking through a hot forest to reach an even hotter clearing.

Before going to my next activity, I felt the need to go back to the hut and cool down. Cyndi Lauper, whose bed was next to mine, asked me what activity I was going to next.

"Riflery," I answered.

"That's where I'm going," Hank chimed in when overhearing us.

A lot of the boys in my hut were headed to riflery. It made sense. We were the hut with the oldest boys in the camp. To take riflery, campers had to be at least thirteen years old and have signed parental permission. This is the first time my mother gave me permission to take riflery. In past summers, she explained to me that I would not like riflery because I was sensitive to loud noises.

Hank went on to talk about how much he enjoyed gun recreation and about when his father had given him his very own gun last year. "I don't believe in guns," Brandon Rhodes was an African American camper in our hut. In later years, it seemed common for African Americans to moral or religious objections to gun possession and use and rare for them to be members of gun ownership rights advocating organizations. I am pretty sure his next activity was not riflery.

Chapter Twelve

The gun range was in a clearing. All of the campers present, including me, chose a rifle. We were all lined up behind a bar. An Aztec was on hand to supervise the session of course but most of my instruction came from a fellow camper. "First you have to load the ammo," he instructed. "That's down here." He pointed to a cubby hole in the bar where there were boxes of bullets. I picked up a box and opened it. "Get one bullet out." I did so and put the box to the side. He told me to open the gun and showed me how to do this and how to load the gun. The gun had a mechanism called a safety. It had to be released before I could fire the gun with the trigger. Upon this camper's instruction, I released the safety and pulled the trigger firing a gun for the first time in my life. The target was a white square with circular red markings and a bull's eye. I hit the target but not near the bull's eye. I thought it was not bad for my first try. I repeated the process of firing the gun several more times following the instructions of the camper who was kind enough to help me. The process each time was load, aim, turn off safety and fire. The crack of my rifle and those of the other participants was loud but bearable for me. I was still sensitive to loud noises more so than the average sixteen-year-old, but I was not nearly as sensitive to them as when I was a small child. After the activity, I walked away very satisfied with my performance considering it was my first time ever.

Next was horseback riding. This was the one activity for which I had to wear jeans. I stopped by the hut long enough to change into some. Then went to a clearing where there were horses and stables. Both the return to the hut from riflery and the walk to the stables were long walks.

An Aztec and a Chippewa were on hand to instruct us on horseback riding. The Aztec introduced himself as Alex and the Chippewa as Annie. Then Alex began instructing us. "The first thing I will talk about is horse safety. It begins even before you get on the horse. Whatever you do, do not walk behind the horse. I made that mistake. The horse kicked me in the leg. This broke my leg. It took three months for me to recover."

Annie then demonstrated the basics of horseback riding. "Always approach and mount the horse from the side." Annie mounted the horse she was working with. She rode the horse briefly while calling attention to how she held the reins and telling us that horses can sense the confidence of their riders. Annie stopped and dismounted. Just as soon as she had gotten off, Annie mounted the horse again and demonstrated what she called an emergency dismount. "Whatever you do, don't scare the horse," she concluded.

We went to the stables to choose horses. I had been horseback riding the two previous years that I had been to camp. That didn't seem like much to me. I had grown up with the impression that no matter how big the city you grow up in, if you are going to grow up out West, then you need to go horseback riding at least once preferably more often. I noticed that familiar dirty but not unpleasant smell of a horse stable. I walked up to one of only two horses that did not have a camper standing next to it indicating that horse was taken. "That's Rocket. He is so sweet," Annie happened to be right behind me and I was startled by her voice. All I wanted was a horse that was manageable.

Our horses were brought out one at a time. All of the campers including myself waited for help from Annie or Alex before mounting our horses. I mounted Rocket. We followed Alex and Annie down a trail on horseback. All of our horses walked at a gentle pace. Occasionally I brushed by tree branches. At one point one of the campers asked if we would do any running. "Not now. We will probably run later," Alex answered.

"Do more of you want to do running?" Alex offered after we had been on the horses longer. "You really have to know what you're doing."

"I'll run," I heard a rider say.

When we got to a clearing there was more talk of running. "Okay. Everyone ready to start running?" After a few seconds, Alex interpreted the lack of response to his question as a lack of objection to running.

I thought that by running they meant that we would get off our horses and run on foot leading our horses with us. Then I realized that it was the horses that would run while we were riding them. When Alex and Annie led their horses to gallop at a running pace, the other horses naturally followed suit. Going at this speed on a horse was a little scary. I did not however plead to stop or cry out in fear. When we got close to the end of the clearing which was also close to the stables, we slowed our horses down and we were walking again. The horses were walking fast though. When we reached the stables, we dismounted.

On my way back to my hut I saw Isabella and Thomas together again. They were looking into each other's eyes intently and walking slowly.

Shortly after I got back to the hut we had three visitors, a boy and his parents. I knew the parents. They were Mr. and Dr. Weiss who taught me at a special summer school program at the University of Portland two years ago. It was after I finished the eighth grade and was about to enter high school. I don't remember the purpose of the program or why I was in it. What I do remember is doing math problems and that there were other students about my age.

"Hi, Tom," Dr. Weiss cheerfully greeted me when she saw and recognized me. "Do you remember me from the Journeys program?" Apparently "Journeys" was the name of the class I was in although I had forgotten that, or perhaps I never picked up on it to begin with.

I assured her that I did remember her.

Then she introduced the boy. "This is our crazy son, Madison. He is starting camp today." I found it odd that he would start camp in the middle of the week, but I didn't say anything.

Madison then went to the only empty cot on our side of the hut and put his baggage by it which included a Casio electronic keyboard.

"Mother, are you sure I have everything?"

"We went over that before we left, I'm sure you will have a good time here."

"Yeah, yeah," Madison's tone of voice reflected a lack of enthusiasm.

Dr. Weiss then turned her attention to me. "How's school?"

"Great."

"We'll be going now but it's good to see you."

"Likewise."

Dr. and Mr. Weiss then walked out of the hut.

That night while we were at an assembly, I met a camper who seemed to be twelve years old at the most. He introduced himself as Raul. We talked about the camp, the good things and the bad things about it. Then he told me one of the camp's spooky legends.

"Have you ever heard the story of Red Jasmine and his cat?" Raul asked me.

"I have to admit that I have not."

I had not heard this story but last year, I had heard one of my hutmates say something very strange and silly and it was cat related. He told some much younger campers that there was an invisible cat with dead bones that would eat stale cake. He then expressed his surprise to us that they actually believed him. He even added that it was a giant cat. One part of the story, on top of the story as a whole being bizarre, did not make sense to me. If the cat was alive, why would the bones inside it be considered dead?

"The story has been around this camp for years. In fact, my parents told me they heard it when they were at camp here. It takes place at Jasmine's Creek and that is where the creek gets its name."

"I'm listening."

"Long ago, Red Jasmine was a camper here. 'Jasmine' was actually his last name. His first name was something like Mike or Mark but everyone at camp called him 'Red' because he had bright red hair, the brightest you have ever seen. Some of the kids made fun of him because of his hair but he found a friend that would not, and in fact, could not judge him. Red befriended a stray cat who wandered onto the camp.

Red later saved a small piece of meat from his lunch to give to the cat. Whenever he got a chance, Red would visit the cat in the patch of woods where it hung out. Eventually the cat started following Red some of the time. Other campers noticed his friendship with the cat and their reaction was mixed. Some of them ridiculed him even more intensely. Others had more respect for him because he was able to get a cat to follow him.

One day, the cat was not following Red. Instead, Red was following the cat. He and the cat went to the edge of the creek not far from the waterfall. Then Red froze when he saw a man on one of the rocks in the rapid part of the creek. The man was a bounty hunter who worked for a crime ring. The bounty hunter was being paid to track down a defector of that crime ring who sneaked away from a meeting that ring was holding. The bounty hunter knew he could not afford to be seen so he aimed his crossbow, the only weapon he had available to him, at Red. The bounty hunter fired an arrow at Red who jumped out of the way. The arrow missed him by less than an inch. In fact, it tore his shirt. Unfortunately, Red's jump was into the rapid waters of the creek. While careening towards the waterfall, Red managed to grab a large stone in the creek and climb onto it. He knew he was risking being shot by the bounty hunter while or after he climbed onto the rock, but the only other choice was to drown. Not very good choices. Are they? Red looked around and did not see the bounty hunter anywhere. Red jumped from rock to rock in the creek hoping to get safely to the bank of the creek and back to camp. Red was on a relatively flat stone surface in the creek and close to shore when he was suddenly grabbed from behind. Nobody is sure why the bounty hunter did not use his crossbow. Maybe he had only that one arrow which he had already shot. Maybe he dropped it in the creek and was unable to get it back. As you can imagine, there was a huge struggle on that stone surface in the creek all while Red's cat watched it. They both fell into the creek and were carried away by a current. They both went over the waterfall and died.

The creek was named Jasmine's creek to honor the camper who tragically died in it. They certainly didn't want to honor the bounty hunter. Sometimes even now you can see a red mist over Jasmine's Creek. Also, you could sometimes see a flash of red reflected in the cat's eyes if you looked at the cat from the right angle."

"What about the defector from the crime ring?"

"He was able to get to the authorities and turn in everyone in the crime ring and they all went to jail."

I was happy to hear that justice prevailed in the story. But I also had the impression that he made up that last part and it was not a part of the myth when it was told to him.

Then Raul showed me a bracelet that was made of interwoven blue and green string. "This is a friendship ring," Raul then put it in my hand. I thanked Raul but I found it odd that he would call me a friend and it was even more peculiar that he considered me a close enough friend to give me something that symbolized that friendship.

I tried to extend the courtesy of continuing the conversation with Raul.

"Where do you live?"

"If you are asking where I'm from, I am from Tacoma."

"What is your family like?"

"I have an older brother in college and two younger sisters. My parents? Well, they're my parents."

The conversation ended when a camper called out to me. "Hey Tom. Do you want to play basketball?" I agreed to join them for basketball. It was one of those player organized games. Campers quickly agreed on who was on each team. It was also half court. Actually, we didn't even use the entire half of the court. This was necessary because of other things going on in the gym on the floor. Some female campers were on the gym floor appearing to try to play hopscotch.

After the game I walked around the gym. I saw Thomas and Isabella again basking in the presence of one another. A minute later, I saw Stacy.

"Uh, hi," I stammered. At this point I was still nervous in Stacy's presence. When a great idea for conversation came into my head, however, the nervousness evaporated.

"Hi," I loved the sweetness and cheerfulness that always colored Stacy's greetings.

"Earlier here in the gym, I was talking to this kid named Raul and he told me this weird ghost story about this camp."

"Really?"

"It's the one about Red Jasmine and his cat."

"I haven't heard that one."

I was surprised.

"Do you want me to tell it to you?"

"Sure."

I retold the story of Red Jasmine to her. Because it took some time to tell her the story, I could tell myself that I had talked to her a long time. I became more and more comfortable with her.

I finished the story just in time because no sooner had I finished, a loud whistle was blown. It was one of the Aztecs who then told us it was time to go back to our huts and get ready for bed.

"Well, I guess that's it," I conceded as Stacy merely nodded in agreement. "Wait a minute. Do you want to me to walk you to your hut?"

"Actually, you can't. Remember the line?"

"I will walk you as far as I can."

"Ok. Thanks."

We walked out of the gym and into the night air outside. Conversation on the way back was not necessary. The enjoyment of the night air and the natural beauty sufficed. Somehow it seemed more beautiful at night even though everything was harder to see. There was no physical contact between Stacy and I, but I kept my hand close to hers in case she wanted to hold it. "You might want to hold my hand, so we won't get separated since it's so dark," I almost made this offer, but I didn't. This practical reason for holding her hand might have been plausible. We got to the closest point to her hut I was allowed to go.

"Good night, Stacy. Don't let the bed bugs bite. And there are some bugs around here that will bite you." When Stacy by laughing lightly and smiling, her soft cheeks stood out. She began walking back to her cabin.

Chapter Thirteen

Thursday, July 4, 1985

Sometime during the morning, we went to the gym for what we were told would be a "presentation." We sat Indian style on the carpeted gym floor. Lane White, one of the adult camp staffers who served as an assistant director, was on the stage and began speaking. "May I have your attention?" The crowd slowly quieted. Then he continued. "We have a great treat for all of you today. I don't know if our guest here has ever been featured on *That's Incredible!* but he certainly should be." Actually, *That's Incredible!* had been cancelled about a year ago. "He has pulled tractors with his teeth, and he holds records for weightlifting. He has performed similar amazing feats at countless venues. He is a committed Christian. Please let me introduce you to Rick Beckram the director of the Lord's Ranch, a children's home dedicated to providing a Christian environment to those who desperately need it."

A very large man walked into view on the stage. He had small eyes or maybe his eyes just seemed small because his head, like the rest of his body, was huge. He had dull red hair. There was a modest amount of applause in the audience.

"Hello everyone," Rick began. After a pause he continued "When you see these feats which I am about to perform, I don't want you to be amazed by me. I want you to be amazed by God. He is the one who gives us all our talents. Without Him, none of us can do anything." A forklift carrying a cube of cinder blocks which was about 1.5 meters tall, wide, and deep laid the cinder blocks on the stage floor. These cinder blocks were surrounded by multiple chains, enough chains so that none of the cinder blocks could come loose. One chain extended outward from the cinder blocks about four meters. Evidently there was a suitable mouthpiece at the end of that extended chain because Rick put the end of the chain in his mouth. Then Rick began walking backwards until the chain was fully tense. After that point it took far more effort on his part. It was several seconds until the cinder blocks budged at all. But eventually we could see it moving. Rick not only got the blocks to move but moved them all the way to the center of the stage. How did I feel when he was performing this stunt? I was worried about his teeth. To me this definitely fell into the "don't try this at home" category.

"Now for my next act, I will need to get this big thing out of the way so you can watch." This meant that he would do something even harder, not just moving the object but changing its direction. The chain was still on the right side of the cube and moving it farther to the right was an option that did not occur to me. This time he used his hands to pull on the chain. Perhaps he was able to move heavy things in one direction with his teeth but was not ready to try to turn an object around with them. Rick pulled hard to his right and very slowly the cube began to turn. Eventually Rick and the chain were on the left side of the blocks. When he had turned the object around 180 degrees, he put his teeth in the mouthpiece and began to pull leftward.

After he had moved the blocks all the way to the left side of the stage, Rick walked back towards the center of the stage while receiving loud applause. He did not bow to us. This would have come across as arrogant or sarcastic. He just lowered his head slightly and clasped his hands together as though to pray and give God the glory. Then Rick stepped aside to make room for an assistant who was already rolling a weight towards him. It was the traditional type of weight with two wheels attached to a bar. This is why he was able to roll it. For Rick to lift it would be a different matter.

"This is 200 pounds," Rick wanted to make sure we knew this.

Then he put his hands on the bar of the weight and gripped it. It took a few seconds, but he quickly moved the weight up and above his head. People cheered. Then he lowered it carefully. Based on my brief experience with weightlifting at the YMCA, I think he had to be quick about lifting the weight before he lost grip of it to gravity. I knew the feeling. My experience with weightlifting was not at all stellar. I was not as good at it as Rick Beckram or most people my age for that matter. I was (and still am) of average height and build and the weight Rick lifted weighed almost twice as much as me! But that was okay. There was a girl at this camp who was attracted to me. *Wow!*

Rick then stood behind the weight and began explaining his organization's mission. "A lot of the kids at the Lord's Ranch came to us because they were fleeing abusive homes. Others were neglected to the point that it was a crime. Sadly, some of our kids were not wanted by their families. Yes, it's all very sad but with the Lord's support, we can help them.

"I know you think I am very strong, but your faith can be just as strong as my body is. Here's how. I have to eat a healthy diet to stay strong and physically fit. You can be spiritually strong when you feed your mind with the right things. Read a biography of a person who was a committed Christian."

Beckram wrapped up his comments and his show by thanking us all for our attention, thanking the camp staff for inviting him, and inviting us to pick up brochures about him and his Lord's Ranch ministry. These brochures were stacked on the edge of the stage, and I was among the people who picked up a copy.

Immediately after the presentation, I stayed in the gym for the activity I was scheduled to attend there. Our activity for the "gym" session was warball. When I arrived at Wininger Gym, kids were walking around aimlessly. One camper was bouncing a white soccer ball off the wall. It was several minutes until an Aztec got us in a left-right line. Again, the team members were chosen by the A-B method in which the Aztec pointed to one camper in line to assign that camper to Team

A and the next camper in line was put on Team B. Again, I was spared the embarrassment of being picked last. Before we started a game both teams decided that the names "Team A" and "Team B" were too dull. "The A Team is a cool show," one camper suggested. "We could call ourselves that." The players on Team A still were not satisfied. Team A, which I was on, decided to call itself the "Warriors." The other team called itself the "Bad Ones."

The other team had the opening throw of the ball. It hit one of our players eliminating him. The ball was then literally in our court. Pete, who was on my team picked it up and tossed it to the other side and missed the opposing player he was apparently aiming the ball at. There were two perpendicular lines marked by tape on the gym floor. The lines were a few feet apart. Both teams were expected to stay out of the area between those lines. Pete was as close to the line on our side as was allowed. The player he was trying to hit was very close to the line on his side too. Yet Pete still missed.

The Bad Ones made three consecutive throws which struck our players. Four on our team were out. None of the Bad Ones had been eliminated. Then there was a fifth member of the Warriors team to go down. *Me.*

I was not happy go have to leave the game so early. Most of my team of thirteen players were still on the court while I walked to sit on the floor Indian Style with the other vanquished players near the wall.

Over half of our team was gone when we finally got one of the guys on the other team. After several more attempts, we got another one. The score, for lack of a better term, was 8-2 at this point. We gained on the other team. For each player they knocked out on our team we would get two of theirs. Eventually there were only two of us and five of them. We managed to eliminate three opponents in a row. It was two on two but just for a brief moment. One of our players was hit with the ball by the other team. We had only one player out there.

"Come on, Jay," was the cheer from one of my teammates. Jay bravely faced the two opponents. He picked up the ball and tossed it at one of the human targets and missed. One of the Bad Ones picked up the ball and hurled it at Jay. It was headed directly towards him, and it missed him by maybe an inch. He retrieved the ball and made a throw which didn't even come close to either of the Bad Ones. After five more unsuccessful tries, Jay finally hit one of the opposing players making it a one-on-one match. The last surviving Bad One got in one of the corners at the far end of the court of play. It was just about impossible for Jay to hit him. Jay did the same thing. Finally, they had to change the rules by shrinking the court. Both players were then reasonably close. It took five more tries but Jay finally grazed the opposing player with the ball. We had won! The Warriors had defeated the bad ones and Jay, a small but agile boy, was the hero.

On the way back to the hut, Cyndi Lauper was talking to me about Rick Beckram. "He was really cool. Wasn't he?"

I simply nodded my head in response.

I took the Lord's Ranch brochure home with me and kept it for several months. A few years later, I saw a report on the local TV news that Rick Beckram was caught committing adultery. His wife had found out by using a private detective.

Back at the hut, Pete asked me a question that made me uncomfortable. As you may recall, Pete is the camper who continually hounded me for my canoeing skills which were not nearly good enough for him when I went canoeing with him earlier in the week. "Let me ask you something. What is it with you? It just seems like you're slow at stuff. I'm not trying to be mean." It was many years until I understood what Pete may have noticed about me and was asking me about.

A moment later, two camp staffers came in our hut. "We just need your radios. You can have them back when camp is over." They had cream colored adhesive tape with them as well as markers to write with. They put a single piece of tape on each radio and wrote the name of the owner of the radio on the tape. As I mentioned earlier, the camp director had reiterated the camp's policy against radios. I was not surprised they were enforcing it. Nor would I have been surprised if they had not enforced it. What seemed odd to me is that they waited two days after his announcement to confiscate the radios.

After they left, our attention turned to another topic. "I have a date to the dance," Jacob had a hint of excitement in his voice.

"I don't have a date yet," Taylor responded. "I am going to ask Kelly next time I see her."

"I already have a date," I chimed in.

"Tom, actually I think I heard Stacy is going with someone else," Cyndi Lauper told me. "It's one of the Cayuses."

Of course, I didn't want this to be true. "She said she would go with me," I told Cyndi Lauper.

"I'm just going by what I heard."

"From whom?"

"I don't remember. You can ask Stacy."

I realized that I had no choice but to do this even though I was very afraid of what I would find out. Nothing hurts worse than romantic jealousy.

Soon I made my way to the gym for my gym activity. "Today we are going to learn the basics of how to dance," the gym Aztec was teaching us. A Chippewa was there to help him instruct.

There was a little bit of irony here. I had arrived at a camp activity in which I would have the opportunity to dance just moments after I had a conversation about whether I would have the opportunity to dance with Stacy.

The dancing they were teaching was not anything I envisioned doing at the dance party with Stacy. We were being instructed to step forward then backwards then sideways all to Bruce Springsteen's "Glory Days." Then again maybe these were the basic elements of dancing, and these steps were part of what I would be doing at the dance party. There was no romance in the class though. Each of the students practiced on their own.

Just after I started crossing the bridge on the way back from this class, I saw Stacy walking the opposite direction toward me. It was a moment of terror because I knew I had to find out the truth about the status of our date.

Chapter Fourteen

"Hi, Stacy."

"Hey, there."

We met each other at around the midpoint of the bridge.

"Can I ask you something?"

"Sure!"

"Are you still going to the dance with me?" My heart braced for the possibility of a crushing rejection.

"Yes. I'm happy to be going to the dance with you, but I want to also dance with some other guys while I'm there," Stacy answered.

"Looking forward to it," then I moved on.

One reason I accepted this is because I had no choice. Another reason is that I remember talking to an older boy in our neighborhood describing going to the prom with his date and he and his date sometimes also danced with partners of the opposite sex at this prom. Based on that, I reasoned that this was normal and customary.

When I got back to the hut, I told Cyndi Lauper about my conversation with Stacy. "Maybe I was right about that dude from the Cayuses." This response from Cyndi Lauper left me wondering if the "other guys" Stacy was talking about was actually just one other guy. It didn't matter though. Either Stacy was going to meet me at that Douglas fir tree, or she would not. Stacy did not say that she had changed her mind about meeting me there and walking with me to the gym as my date.

Later that day shortly after lunch, Madison walked into the hut looking angry. "I can't believe it," he also sounded angry. "Doug is dead. I tell you he's dead. I was standing in front of Lana, and I was about to ask her to be my date for the dance and then Doug asked her to be his date and she said 'sure.'" Lana O'Callaghan was a moderately attractive Hawaiian girl who was, like my beloved Stacy Sapp, a camper in the Tenino hut. Doug was a warm, charming twelve-year-old small boy.

Madison continued his rant. "That makes me so mad, I feel like I'm going to explode. I really ought to knock his teeth down his throat. Wait a minute. That's too good for him. He should be dead." In today's world, these words would have resulted in a police investigation even though they were the words of a fifteen-year-old camper. This however was the 1980's.

"Were you really going to ask her out?" Logan tried to understand and resolve the situation.

"Yes! I was seconds away from it. He knew I was about to ask her."

"Maybe you can find another girl to ask."

"I could but Doug shouldn't get away with this."

"Did he interrupt you?"

"Yes!"

"What were you saying before you were about to ask her out?"

"I don't remember."

I had my doubts as to whether Madison was telling the truth. Madison picked up his Casio keyboard. I would not have been surprised if he hurled it across the cabin. Thankfully he didn't. Instead, he snarled, "This is going to be his dead song."

I left the hut. I was genuinely concerned that Madison was going to hurt somebody. Dick who was one of the camp staff members walked by, so I told him about my concern.

"Madison is really upset. He says he is going to kill Doug."

"Madison is just talking," Dick replied. "You can't always believe what he is saying. He really likes to mouth off."

Satisfied, I went back into the hut.

In light of Madison's tirade, I felt fortunate to have a date. "Maybe you can talk to Benjamin Heimer and ask him what to do." I was trying to be a friend to Madison in spite of his sour mood.

"Who's he? Wait, he's the director. Leave the director out of it," was Madison's reply.

I don't know why I thought that was a good idea. Maybe it was because Benjamin Heimer was a good friend to my family and me. I guess I forgot that may not be the case with all of the other campers.

"You could talk to Adam or Bobby about it. I know we call them leaders, but they are actually counselors. That means you can talk to them about whatever is on your mind."

"I'll deal with it myself. Thank you." Madison did not seem as self-confident as that statement would suggest.

The next activity was swimming. As I headed towards the pool, some girls stopped me. They seemed to be the right age to be in Stacy's hut. "Are you really taking Stacy to the dance?" one of them seemed delighted by the idea and wanted to confirm it.

"Uh, yes?"

"That's so sweet!"

Getting in the pool was very refreshing after a day of sweaty activities. It was not a swimming contest or a swimming lesson. We could do whatever we wanted in the water. While I splashed about in the pool, I used the time to think about all that had transpired since I arrived at Camp Sunbeam. I entered a new relationship with Jesus. I fired a gun for the first time ever. I met an awesome girl who found me attractive. Most recently, I witnessed an unfortunate meltdown by one of my hut mates regarding a dispute over a girl. Tomorrow I would go on my first date ever.

After dinner, Bobby called a meeting of all of us in the hut. I noticed that there were fourteen campers among us, not all fifteen. "I have something very important to talk to you about." Bobby began. "This is something not to be discussed outside this hut." Even though the sun had not set, it seemed dark in the hut. "Dan got caught smoking again," Bobby continued. I did not remember hearing about the first time he got caught smoking. "He is the one who brought the guitar.

Dan is very talented but also very troubled. Dan needs our help bad."

"But how can we help him? What can we do?" The question came from Taylor, but it was the same thought I had.

"Accept him. Be nice to him. Do not exclude Dan from anything. He will probably still smoke but he will be less likely to smoke or do even more self-destructive things if he feels accepted by his peers. Finally, be the best example around him as possible. The camp staff is going to talk to Dan's parents, but first they are going to talk to Dan himself. His relationship with his parents may be strained. His parents may be smokers themselves."

I did not bring it up, but this reminded me of an incident yesterday. Dan asked me to do him a favor and buy him a Coke while we were all at Oasis. I wondered, but did not ask Dan, why he did not buy it himself. I told him that I only had enough money to buy my own snack and drink from Oasis.

I was aware that Oasis is a privilege that is sometimes taken away from campers as a disciplinary act. Based on what I heard at this meeting, it occurred to me that maybe Dan could not get his own Coke because he was being denied Oasis because he was being punished for smoking. Maybe he was being punished for something else.

"Well, I think smoking is disgusting," Mark had a sick expression on his face.

"Agreed, but that is not the point," was Bobby's rational response. "The point is that smoking is against camp policy. At the same time, we want to be able to provide Dan with the best guidance possible. We can only do that if he's here at camp."

There were no other questions or comments.

That night even after the lights were turned out in our hut, my hut mates continued conversing as though the day were not over. I got the feeling something was about to happen.

"Do you hear that?" Mark alerted us. "I think there are some guys outside."

"What makes you think that?" Ryan wanted a reason to be suspicious.

"Didn't you hear that? It sounded like people walking around. I think it's some of the Cayuses."

"Or they could be Pawnees." The Pawnees were a boys' hut whose members were on average slightly younger than the Cayueses.

"Maybe it's a wolf," Juan chimed in.

"A wolf?" was Mark's reaction. "Maybe if we just all stay quiet, we can tell what is going on out there and if there is anything we need to do, we'll do…"

Mark did not get to finish his sentence because a huge amount of water was thrown through the screens of our hut and onto our beds. In our cabins at camp, we did not have glass windows, just screens. This was a sudden cold shock to me. I got wet. Even the bed sheets had some water on them after this happened. The water went on several other campers on my side of the cabin too. I heard a camper on my side of the hut cuss. Even some of the guys in unaffected areas of the cabin started grumbling.

"Calm down. We'll get back at them later," Adam reassured us.

The lights were still off so I don't know which camper said what, but this is what I heard as several of them spoke.

"It was the Cayuses."

"How can you be so sure?"

"I saw them walking back to their hut. That is bold even for them. They are dead maggot meat."

"Any ideas?" It was clear that this speaker was asking about ideas for revenge.

"I have some bug spray. We could spray it through their windows. It would be appropriate since they're pests."

"I will pee in a cup. The rest of you can contribute too."

"Let's just make it an eye for an eye. We will use just as much water as they used to attack us, but it will just be water. We will need a container, maybe several containers."

I was not participating in the planning session, for lack of a better term, but I was listening and thinking about each idea that was brought up. I was okay with the idea of getting back at them, but I had many questions about how we could go about doing it. I could not think of any containers. We didn't have any buckets in the hut. I don't even think any of us even had any cups in the hut. We normally didn't drink anything that would be poured into a cup while in the hut. The only exception to that was our leaders who occasionally had cans of Coke or Dr. Pepper or something like that in their quarters and sometimes they preferred to pour it in a cup. Even if we had cups, or better yet, a bigger container of some sort, whoever was tasked with filling it up would have to go to a separate building where there were sinks, toilets, and showers. None of these things were in our cabin. In fact, the only utility going into our cabin was electricity.

A few minutes later several of the guys walked to Adam's tiny room. They were apparently going over retaliation ideas with Adam. "Water's legal," I heard Adam say. Several minutes later the talking that seemed to come from the common room stopped. The common room is the room the front door of the hut opens into. None of the beds were in there. Instead, there were a few built-in benches people could sit on. I felt sure that the plotters sat on these benches when they were collaborating. A few minutes after that, I thought I saw silhouettes and heard light voices and rustling when looking out the screen window by my bed.

A few minutes later, I heard a few hut mates come back in our hut. Taylor, who was one of the ones who came back in the hut, settled into his bed which was two beds from mine. "Did you get 'em?" Logan asked Taylor.

"Yeah, but it was no big deal to them. Even after we dumped the water on them, we had to say 'Ha, ha! Got you!' to get their attention. It seems like we went through a lot of trouble for almost nothing."

"Maybe you missed."

"What do you mean?"

"The water may not have gotten on their beds like it did ours. It may have just been on the floor. How did you do it?"

"We figured that the floor in the bathhouse needed to be mopped and that there would be a bucket somewhere in there. Sure enough, we found a closet, probably used by the janitor, where there was a bucket. We filled it with water. Since it was a bucket full of water, it should have gotten their attention. We were going to tell the rest of this hut to watch out for another attack, but I don't think it's coming." No other attack came that night.

Soon I was both physically and mentally settled into my bed and was reflecting on the day. What seemed peculiar about that day was that even though it was Independence Day a.k.a. the Fourth of July, it was for the most part like any other day at camp. One of the camp staffers gave a speech at lunch related to the Fourth and our country's struggle for independence. I also heard a camper in passing say "Happy Fourth of July." But the camp did not put on any fireworks show or take us to such a show. Last year I had gone to a place where I got a great view of the fireworks show back home but this year, I missed the fireworks because I was at camp. There were no Fourth of July themed or America themed programs held by the camp. On the other hand, I could say that I was celebrating independence by being at camp away from my family and in a sense making it on my own.

Chapter Fifteen

Friday, July 5, 1985

It was Friday, Date Day. It was the day on which I would go on my first date. It was to be my final day of activities at camp but the date with Stacy Sapp stood out in my mind. I couldn't shake the feeling that something could go wrong. What if Stacy didn't show up at the Douglas fir tree at the time we agreed to? Sure, she might be a little bit late but what if she didn't show up at all? A friend of mine at school told me that there was a term for that. It was called "being stood up." Even worse, what if she showed up with another guy? Jealousy hurts like crazy. I would have to see her at the dance with that other guy. But none of this had happened yet and might not happen at all. I decided to be happy that I had a date and while I was at it, I would enjoy the other camp activities too.

The first of those activities would be basketball. It was what we were told yesterday we would be doing in the gym. Since there were ten boys and eight girls, it was decided that the boys would play five-on-five, the minimum number of members on each team for it to be true basketball, on one end of the court and the girls would play four-on-four on the other end. This time I was spared from the team picking ritual. The Aztec in charge used a random method to put us on teams. When the game started, I was point guard which is the closest thing that basketball has to a quarterback in football. I was at the top of the key. "Top of the key" when used in basketball means that I was almost at half court distance from the goal and all of the other players were closer to the goal. It was up to me who to pass the ball to. I could also go in and try to score myself. I passed it to a player to my left.

It was not until seven possessions later that I was again point guard. The position was taken by a different player each time. I made an ill-advised pass to a player very close to the goal. He didn't lose the ball but was in a position in which he was trapped by opposing players and could not go anywhere. Finally, he managed to get the ball passed to a player who was not trapped. That player in turn passed it to me. But missed by what seemed like a mile. Not only did the pass miss me but the ball went all the way to the other side of the court where the girls were playing. The ball kept flying but eventually started bouncing. It was still headed away from me. The basketball bumped into the leg of one of the girls. That girl did the polite thing. She picked up the ball so she could hand it to me. I approached her so she could give me the ball. Then I was surprised and excited to see who the girl was. *Stacy Sapp.*

When Stacy recognized me, she greeted me with the standard polite "Oh, hi."

Stacy handed me the ball. The girls' game of course had paused. The other girls smiled in amusement, and I thought I heard a giggle among the girls. They were starting to tease her about her budding romance with me. I simply thanked her for the ball and went back to my side of the court. I almost reminded Stacy "See you at the dance," but the girls would have shown no mercy.

Back at the hut before we went to lunch, there was an incident that bothered me. I saw what Bobby had talked to us about yesterday. Dan was smoking right in front of me. "Stop it," I was also expressing my disapproval by waving the smoke away from my face.

"Fine, I'll go somewhere else," Dan departed to the other side of the hut before I could tell him that smoking is unhealthy which was probably the whole idea.

When we went to lunch there was a considerably long wait. I thought of it as not necessarily a bad thing but an opportunity I might be able to use to my advantage. When my hut mates and I were outside the mess hall waiting for the doors to open, I saw Stacy behind me in the crowd which included not only those in my hut but people from other huts as well. It was not really a line. It was more like a mob waiting to get in. She was with other girls presumably from her hut. I had a decision to make. I thought it might be wise to remind her of the place where we agreed to meet before walking to the dance together. But doing this presented a terrifying possibility. What if she told me that she had changed her mind about going to the party with me? I would be crushed. I would probably burst into tears right in front of her and her friends. I had to take this risk though. Even a girl with full intentions of going on a date with me could forget the details. Also, when we agreed to meet fifteen minutes before the dance, we did not know the exact time of the event. This morning at breakfast it was announced that the dance party would be at 8:00 pm. I needed to make sure Stacy understood this. I made my way back through the crowd of campers until I got to Stacy. As I did so, I felt the chill of terror at the possibility of her bailing on me.

"Hi, Stacy," I finally reached her in the crowd.

"Oh, hi."

"Do you remember where we are going to meet before the dance tonight?"

"A Douglas fir tree, right."

"Do you know which Douglas fir tree?" The fact that she said "a" before "Douglas fir" caused me to be concerned that she was not sure which one and there might be more than one Douglas fir tree in the common area between the set of boys' huts and the set of girls' huts.

"It's the one you showed me, the one between all the huts." If we were not all about to have to go to lunch, I would have considered walking her to the tree again out of an abundance of caution. Nonetheless, I was confident that she would see me on her way from her hut to the gym. Either that or I would see her. Her hut was visible from this tree.

"Right," I answered her. "Oh yeah and the dance party is at 8:00 tonight so we will meet at the tree at 7:45."

"Okay."

I was relieved that this conversation was behind me now. Satisfied that she would be there, I rejoined my hut mates in the crowd. I joined them just in time too. Just as I got back to my peers, the doors to the mess hall opened and people started moving forward and going in.

After lunch we were resting in the hut. The campers were talking about what kind of music they hoped would be at the dance. Then Pete changed the subject slightly. "I thought about asking Karen to the dance, but I decided against it. When I was talking to her the other day, she started talking about Strawberry Shortcake. That's for little babies."

Then Cyndi Lauper chimed in. "I think Tom here is just about the only one who has a date." This comment made me feel a little bit self-conscious and guilty for wanting a date. If it were true, then everyone else was able to be happy without a date yet I was insisting on having one. I realize now and I realized then that there was no need to feel this way because I was doing nothing wrong. I did not act on these feelings in any way.

Dan started talking to me about something that was not only a little off the subject. It was way off the subject. "I'm sorry. I didn't know that you were sensitive to smoke."

I appreciated the apology, but he was missing the point. I didn't want him to smoke because smoking is consistently bad for your health. Junk food is bad for you too, but it is okay in strict moderation. On the other hand, no amount of tobacco is safe. "It's not that. You shouldn't smoke," is how I expressed these feelings in words. "Why do you smoke?" I thought I could get to the root of the problem there.

"It's just a habit!"

But it was more than just a habit. It was an addiction. I remember hearing on a radio news station about a scientific study providing evidence that cigarettes contain nicotine which provide comfort to the brain and has a calming effect. According to the study, smokers feel like they need the nicotine regularly.

If there was anything I could have done to help Dan at that moment, I would have done it in a heartbeat. Maybe I was wrong, but I could not think of a thing I could do for him. I decided I might as well mentally prepare for my hot date tonight and enjoy the activities before that.

When I left the hut and went to my swimming activities, I waded and relaxed in the pool while wondering about what it would feel like to slow dance with Stacy. The mere thought of her and this date made every nerve in my body light up with excitement. For my other two activities that afternoon, I had to put Stacy out of my mind. Riflery and horseback riding were things that had to be done very carefully. I knew it was important to keep my balance on the horse and not to have any accidents when handling guns or bullets.

When we went to the mess hall for dinner, I had on the same blue jeans and raggedy T-shirt that I had worn to horseback riding. I knew I would have to change when I got back to the hut after dinner. After dinner several of us including myself showered off in the bath house. I changed into a T-shirt and shorts just enough so I could walk from the bath house to the hut decently dressed. I didn't want to put my horseback riding T-shirt and jeans back on. I didn't want to dirty myself up with those dirty clothes after I had just gotten clean in the shower. When I got back to the hut, I looked through my suitcase for the nicest outfit I could find. I found some khaki shorts and a green short sleeve collared shirt. My mother had taught me about color coordination. Certain colors looked better together. They did not have to be the same color. In fact, it was often better if the colors were not the same. A shirt and pants of different colors went together well just as long as the colors did not clash. I once asked my mother about a shirt and pants which I was wearing, which were of radically different colors, "Does this outfit clash?"

Her answer was, "No. It wages all-out war."

It didn't matter if the shirt looked right with my shorts. It was the only shirt I had that was not a T-shirt. I had included it in my packing just in case I went to some nice event. I was very thankful I had. I could be forgiven for not having a coat, tie, dress button down shirt, and dress pants packed for summer camp, but I wanted to wear something nicer than a T-shirt for my first date. I was also glad that I rinsed the mud off my sneakers right after the caving event earlier this week. I put them on after I put on some clean white socks.

I not only got dressed but I also combed my hair. I had a comb packed as well. It was something my mother insisted that I pack, and it was something else I am glad I packed. In fact, one of the other boys asked to borrow my comb. I was in front of the mirror in Adam's small room to comb my hair. This was the only mirror in the hut. When I looked at my hair and the rest of myself in this mirror, I was pleased. I was also glad that I did not have any pimples that week. I noticed Adam's deodorant in his quarters and thought about asking him if I could use it. But I decided that since I had just showered that I was clean and there was no risk of smelling bad.

I walked back to my cot. It was 7:25 pm and there were still twenty minutes until time to meet Stacy at the tree. These twenty minutes seemed like an eternity. I could have walked to the meeting point right then, but I didn't want to be awkwardly early. If I wanted to wait while feeling the mixture of excitement and anxiety that I was feeling, I would rather do so in the hut with my hut mates some of whom were also preparing for dates. I would leave at 7:40 which would give me time to walk towards the tree and probably have some time to spare. I didn't think it would take more than two minutes to walk there. So actually, it would be fifteen minutes that I would have to wait. I sat on my cot and talked to Cyndi Lauper whose bed was next to mine.

"You look snazzy in that outfit," he began the conversation.

"Thanks."

"Do you think there will be good music at this dance?"

I was just hoping I would get through my date even if the music was lousy. I was also hoping there would be at least one slow song so I could slow dance with Stacy.

"I don't know."

The verbal exchange drifted to other activities at the camp. It lasted until Bobby came in the room and told us that it was almost time to go. I checked my wristwatch. *7:37 pm.* It was just about time for *me* to go. It occurred to me that I needed to talk to Bobby or Adam about my plans. I would not be walking down with the others to the gym. I don't know how many others at camp were planning to meet their dates at a special place and then walk to the dance party.

"Bobby," I called to get his attention and then walked to him. "I need to go meet my date to the dance and walk to it with her."

"We will all be going down to that in a few minutes."

"But I told her I would meet her under a certain tree in the, uh, common area." I used the phrase "common area" because I could not think of a good term for the area between the guys' huts and the girls' hut. I was suddenly afraid that Bobby would not let me meet Stacy under the Douglas fir tree. If that happened, I would not be there when Stacy got there, and she would think that I stood her up. She would walk to the gym angry and sad. She would see me, and I could then explain that I was not allowed to be there. She would understand. If she didn't understand, then she was not a good romantic partner anyway. Still, I wanted to meet Stacy under the Douglas fir tree so it would all go smoothly.

"Just join us as soon as you meet her."

"Okay, thank you." I was so relieved that I would be able to meet her there that I sighed as I spoke.

I walked out of Bobby's quarter and out of the hut. Before I walked to the tree, I took a detour. I went to a place not far from the bridge where I saw a small naturally occurring plant. The flowers were tiny, and white with a gold tip. I picked off a small part of the plant and even though it was just a small part, there were eight little flowers on it. Then I began my beeline walk to the Douglas fir tree. As I made my way to the tree, I began to feel the butterflies in my stomach. This only increased as I got closer to the tree. Once I was there, I was still excited, but I was relaxed. I had made it there in the nick of time. It was 7:44 in the evening (though the sun was still up).

I looked in the direction of Stacy's hut and then at my wristwatch just as 7:45 came. I was conscious of the exact minute we were to meet because of the huge importance of the event. A moment later two girls passed but neither of them was Stacy. Then a younger boy walked by. I hated every time that a person walked by and was not Stacy. Only a few minutes had passed but of course it seemed much longer than that.

I thought about how long I should stay at the tree if she didn't show up. How much time should I give her? Maybe I would start heading down if Stacy was fifteen minutes late. Maybe I would give her twenty minutes. I decided on fifteen minutes which would be 8:00 since my hut leaders and the others were expecting me to go to the event even if I didn't walk with them. I didn't think my hut leaders wanted me to stay under the tree all night. If Stacy didn't show up and I had to go on to the dance and Stacy showed up at the dance afterwards, I could explain that I waited fifteen minutes after our meeting time and had to go on to the party to avoid being too late. The only way Stacy would not show up at the dance at all is if she somehow got sick or had some other genuine emergency. Or maybe she would fake sick so she would have an excuse not to go to the dance with me. She might do that if she was shy enough. I would be very hurt if she did this. I checked my wristwatch. *7:50 pm.*

Then a larger number of people came out of Stacy's hut which I could see in the distance. Even if one of them was Stacy, it would take her at least a minute to get here. It was four girls following a slightly older one who I think was their hut leader. None of them was Stacy but there were two other girls behind them, one of whom was being helped by the other girl because she appeared unable to walk on her right leg. Stacy had apparently hurt her ankle. My heart sank. This is the absolute worst thing that can happen to someone I am supposed to dance with at a party. This was my first date and I felt like I couldn't afford for Stacy to have any excuse not to dance with me or be my date. It was as though the gods of romance, luck, and health were conspiring against me.

Chapter Sixteen

"I t'll be fine," the girl with Stacy told her. "Just keep using that foot. Dance on it." It was hard for me to tell if the girl was serious. Most likely she was half serious.

"Hi, Stacy," was all I could say as I joined the girls and walked to the gym with them. My date was officially under way. Though the circumstances were very different from what I had pictured, I had met Stacy at the meeting point, walked with her to the event, and had arrived there.

It was not until this time did I give Stacy the flower. "Thank you. It's pretty," Stacy reacted. She took the flower gently with her hand. I sensed that her overall reaction was typical of someone who had just received a small gift. She truly appreciated it and also liked it but was not overwhelmed by it. Stacy seemed puzzled as to what to do with the flower. She did not have a purse or locker to put it in. Running back to her hut would have been awkward and time consuming even if her feet were both healthy. It was that much further out of the question with her hurt ankle.

"Put it in your hair," I hoped I sounded like I was giving her a suggestion and not a command.

"It will fall out."

"Not if you put it by your ear."

In the end she decided to put the flower in a place in the gym where it was unlikely to be noticed by any of the other campers. I thought about offering to put it some place for her because of her ankle, but she would have had to follow me to wherever I put it so she would know where it was and would have ended up having to walk anyway.

By the time Stacy got back to me, the music had started. It was a fast upbeat song that was not really danceable. None of the other campers were dancing. We just stood and enjoyed listening to the song. Isabella joined us. I had seen her come in with Thomas as her date, but he was not around.

"Do you like the food here?" I started this conversation because I felt like I needed to get to know Stacy better at every opportunity.

"It's okay."

"We had pizza one night."

"Yeah, but it was that gross kind of pizza like what we have at school."

"Do you expect Pizza Hut?"

"I expect it to be edible."

"Do you miss home cooking?"

"Oh yes. My Mother's cooking is great. She also works at the school cafeteria."

"The school you're going to?"

"No, the elementary school."

The conversation ended when a song which was fast paced and easy to dance to started playing. "Want to dance?" I pounced on the opportunity to dance with Stacy.

"Okay."

She started dancing and I took her hands and began to dance with her.

"We don't have to hold hands," Stacy still seemed happy to dance with me.

I wish I had asked her if it was okay if we did hold hands. I let go of her hands. We would dance close but with no physical contact at least for this song. For about three minutes we celebrated life by dancing. We both had great families. Unlike the people in some other parts of the world my hut mates and I were singing about on our first day of camp during our "We Are the World" skit, we had plenty of food and other necessities and were materially blessed even beyond that. We lived in a free country. Maybe I was just having all of these happy thoughts because fast dancing put me in a good mood.

After this song, Stacy and I briefly walked around the gym just to see what the others were doing. Some of the campers were dancing. Others were just standing around talking to each other. I saw a boy and girl who looked to be old enough to be in college. They were looking at each other as though there were a slow song playing, they would not only be dancing but they would be dancing very close. When we were walking, Stacy was slowed down by her hurt ankle. I offered to help, and she accepted. I was happy to put my arm between her arm and her side and help her get around. We found a space in the midst of the crowd where we could both stand easily and hang out. There was a fast Michael Jackson song playing. The song was about two or three years old, but it was still popular. But the song was nearing its end and we only danced to it for a few seconds.

Then my luck changed from good to fantastic. A slow song began to play. It was Journey's "Open Arms." We just looked at each other and blushed slightly with our heads pointed slightly down. I motioned to begin dancing with Stacy. And she cooperated! We put our arms around each other's backs, and I put my head by her head. Within seconds my nose was in her light brown wavy hair. *Pure magic!*

We were dancing on a thin green carpet which served as the gym's floor. There was no special lighting for the event. It was the same harsh white gym lights on the ceiling that were there for basketball, volleyball, official gatherings, etc. I felt as though these surroundings went black. They didn't matter. The other dancers, the campers, and the camp staff might as well have not been there. All that mattered was this special moment which I had no idea would happen when I arrived at camp at the beginning of the week. Her hair smelled good, and I was not sure why. Was it shampoo? Was it just the natural smell of her hair? Then she broke her silence.

"I'm sorry."

I had no idea, nor could I imagine, what there was for her to apologize for. If she was apologizing because I was not having a good time, nothing could be farther from the truth.

"You're sorry for what?" I asked gently.

"I have to stop. My foot is hurting too much." There was genuine sadness in her voice.

I knew what this meant. She had to stop dancing with me. I slowly and gently let go of her body. Stacy went to the gym wall and sat down. I stood there not knowing what to think or do. I felt sad and isolated. Others around me had someone to dance with but I didn't. When this song ended, a fast dance song began. Then I walked to where Stacy was. Isabella was with her.

"I'll dance with you," Isabella offered.

"Are you sure Thomas wouldn't mind if I danced with you?"

She shook her head quickly. We danced right then and there. She wanted me to have someone to dance with. I thought this was very kind of her. It was a fast upbeat song. Isabella danced in front of me as I danced in front of her. She snapped her fingers a few times while moving her feet to the music. I made it a point to have fun at that moment. She was being a good friend to me. Nonetheless it was Stacy who was special to me. This was the first time I had romantic feelings for a girl and there was a reasonably good chance that she felt the same way about me. I will never forget how exciting this was.

After my dance with Isabella, I went to the gym wall to talk to Stacy.

"Hi, Stacy," I began.

"Hey."

"Are you nervous about going into high school?"

"Not really."

"What are you going to study?"

"Well, I know I'll have to take Washington (state) history and English and I will take algebra."

"Any favorites?"

"I am looking forward to foreign languages though I don't think I will take any this year. My personal favorite is French."

"Pardon my French."

She got the joke. It is something people say when they are about to say cuss words. She giggled lightly and I loved the way her cheeks stuck out whenever she laughed or smiled.

Why did I crack a joke? I had heard countless times that one of the biggest things that a girl likes in a guy is a sense of humor.

"Actually, I will probably end up taking German," Stacy continued the conversation. This was ironic because German was actually the foreign language that I studied the following school year. I was about to become a high school junior. Stacy was about to be a high school freshman.

"Are you going to play any sports?"

"Not play sports but I will be in the band at the football games."

A slow song began playing. I would have loved to have danced with Stacy to this song, but I didn't want to ask her to dance with me with her foot hurting this much. Our conversation continued. She talked about her hobbies and interests. I learned more about her family including her non-immediate family. Stacy mentioned that she had a grandmother in Portland.

Later I went out to dance when they were playing a fast song that I particularly liked and seemed like a song that was easy to dance to. Then I spent some time hanging out with my cabin mates.

"Are you having a good time with Stacy?" Cyndi Lauper was being a true friend by wanting to know if my date was going well.

"Sure. She can't dance much because of a hurt ankle, but I'm having a good time with her. I think I'd better check on her now."

I turned to go to where Stacy was when I was last talking to her. Stacy was not there. I looked all over the gym for Stacy, but she was nowhere to be seen. The dance party was almost over, and a few people had gone back to their huts, particularly the younger campers. However, I had thought that since this was a date, we would go to the dance together (which we did) and that we would come home from the dance together. By "home" I mean our huts. I envisioned myself taking Stacy as far towards her hut as was allowed by the invisible line between the boys' huts and the girls' huts. When I finished walking with her back towards her hut, I was dreaming that I might even work up the courage to ask her if I could kiss her goodnight.

I had been sad that Stacy couldn't dance with me much. Now I was sad again because I could not find her at all. Soon Adam got all the Shoshones together and we went back to the cabin to get ready to go to bed.

After lights out, I was thinking about Stacy. I wondered if I would see her again. My time with Stacy had been great but it was likely over now. I did not know if I would get a chance to see her tomorrow. Maybe I would see her at breakfast, the last breakfast of my week at camp. She had sent so many mixed signals as to whether she was interested in me. Then I had a horrible thought. What if Stacy was faking her ankle injury so she would have an excuse not to dance with me? Sometimes young girls can be shy and that can make them do things like that. Then again, she was not too shy to ask me to sit by her in the Rotunda. Besides, she did dance with me some and she could have used the injury, real or not, as an excuse not to dance with me at all. Would we have any relationship after camp? I did not have any of Stacy's contact information. I knew her hometown but not her address.

Chapter Seventeen

Saturday, July 6, 1985

I got up in the morning of my last day at camp for this week at least. Later that morning my mother or father or both would pick me up and take me home. That day I was on a mission. I had to find Stacy Sapp before she or I went home. I would have loved to have gone to the Tenino hut and knocked on the door and asked to see Stacy but as I mentioned before, I was not allowed to do that. I hoped to see her in line for breakfast right outside the Mess Hall or in the Mess Hall during breakfast. The latter was probably not an option even if I saw Stacy in the Mess Hall because there seemed to be an unwritten rule: Nobody leaves the table. I would probably have to hope that Stacy left breakfast at almost exactly the same time that I did so that I could catch her on the way back to the huts.

When we got to the Mess Hall for breakfast, we all went right in. There was not a crowd gathered at the door to get in because the door was open. This was one time I was actually unhappy that we did not have to wait to get into the hall to eat. If there had been a crowd by a yet-to-be-opened door, maybe Stacy would be in that crowd.

We were served pancakes at breakfast. This was the only day all week that we were served something sweet for breakfast. Maybe they wanted to give us a treat since this was our last day. The pancakes were delicious, but I wanted Stacy. I looked around the hall hoping to see her at one of the other tables. I saw a girl who looked like she might be Stacy in the other corner of the room.

The conversation taking place among my hut mates did not seem important at the time but soon was important.

"Do they really have the Oasis open right now?" Cyndi Lauper asked.

"Yeah, they want us to have that last opportunity to get stuff before we go."

It occurred to me that maybe Stacy would be at Oasis, so I began formulating plans in my mind to go there after breakfast. The chances of seeing her there were not good, but it seemed like I was much more likely to see her there one more time before I went home than if I simply went back to the hut after breakfast.

When we were mostly finished eating, Dylan raised his glass of milk and announced, "A toast to the last supper." I was mostly puzzled. Even though we were eating breakfast, not supper, it was our last meal. Fair enough. He also may have been thinking of the Last Supper which Jesus (whose salvation I had accepted just a few days earlier) had with his apostles as mentioned in the Bible. I had seen a picture of a famous painting of the Last Supper in a textbook at school. But why did he say "toast"? Toast was not a part of our meal. We just had scrambled eggs, sausage, and pancakes.

Then he touched Hank's glass of milk. Hank had raised his glass a well. We all did. I also raised my glass eventually because everyone else at the table was doing it. Then I wondered if we were playing pig. It didn't matter. Although I was late in raising my glass, I wasn't the last. Then it became clear that we were not playing pig because the last camper at the table to raise his glass was not assigned pig duties. Later Hank put his spoon on his nose, a classic pig move. We all quickly followed suit with the last one of us to do so being assigned pig duties (It wasn't me). When the assistant pig round came, I was purposely in last place and told the whole table, "I volunteer to be assistant pig." I did so to avoid being assigned floor duty in the third and final round. As assistant pig, I would be finished before everyone left the table. But to sweep the floors, I would have had to wait until all of the campers had left the table. I did not want to risk this extra delay in getting to the Oasis. Increasing my chances of seeing Stacy Sapp one more time was that important.

After all of the campers at the table were finished, I walked with the camper who had won (or rather lost) pig duty and brought back a big tray to put the plates and glasses in. We then took them back to the kitchen and rinsed them. After this, I immediately walked to the Oasis. I envisioned a long line at the Oasis which would hopefully include Stacy. When I got there, however, there was no line at all, but the store was open. I would not have even walked up to the open window where things are sold if I had not spotted an item I wanted. It was a green T-shirt with "Camp Sunbeam" and a small series of trees on it. I asked the woman at the window for that shirt in my size. The woman left the window and was out of view for a while. I felt impatience. Every second I waited there made it more likely that Stacy would be gone from camp by the time I got back to my hut and figured out a way to see her one last time. Finally, the woman showed up with a copy of the T-shirt I ordered and quoted the price to me. I reached into my pocket and opened up my wallet and paid in cash. The shirt was in a plastic bag. She also tried to give me change but I was gone as soon as the bag was in my hand. I didn't even say "Keep the change."

I moved as quickly back to my hut as I could without attracting the attention of a camp staff member who would say "No running." When I walked into our hut, the mood was festive with a little bit of sadness mixed in based on this being our last few moments together. There were girls from the girls' huts in our hut. I guess this late in the camp session it didn't matter. Relief and exhilaration hit me when I saw who was sitting on one of the beds in my wing of the hut. *Stacy!*

"Hi!" Stacy's voice was cheerful. Isabella, who was sitting next to Stacy, also greeted me.

"Well, I guess this is it," I conceded.

"Do you want my address?" Stacy asked me.

"Oh good, yes." I had trouble articulating how happy I was that we would be able to stay in touch. This romance was too special to let die.

"Oops! I don't have anything to write it on," Stacy noticed after getting her pen out of her purse.

I had to find a piece of paper somewhere. This was too important. It seemed like my best bet was Bobby. I went to his very small room, and I didn't have to ask him if he had anything to write addresses on. Bobby was already giving his address on a small notepad piece of paper to one of the other campers. I thought about asking for his address as well but after a few seconds of thought, I decided to concentrate on my first priority, getting contact information from Stacy Sapp. I politely asked Bobby for a piece of the notepad paper, and he was happy to give it to me. It was a yellow piece of paper ruled with blue lines. I took it and made my way back to Stacy. I eagerly handed Stacy the piece of paper. She looked around for a place to put the paper against to write on it. She eventually had to settle for using her knee for this purpose. Stacy gently handed me the golden contact information. I examined it.

Stacy Sapp
Route 3, Box 27
Lakota, Wash. 98678

Then I folded it and put it in my wallet.

"Thank you," I responded. "I will write you a letter and I will do it soon."

"Give me a hug," Stacy opened her arms for one. I happily obliged and we hugged tightly. If we had been alone, I might have asked her if she wanted a kiss but even at that awkward age, I knew that would probably embarrass her. A kiss would come in time if it was meant to happen at all.

"You can give me one too," Isabella offered.

"Give you what?"

"A hug."

So, I gave Isabella a hug.

I had already packed my suitcase before breakfast so all I had to do was get the suitcase and walk out the door and look for Mother or Dad. When I walked out the door of the hut and turned the corner, I saw Mother roughly ten meters away. She greeted me enthusiastically. We walked together back to the car. On the way, we caught up to Ray.

"Is this your mother?" Ray asked me.

"Yes!"

Ray then introduced himself to my mother.

"Have you had a good time this week?" my mother asked Ray.

"Yeah, pretty good."

"Where are you from?"

"Portland. We live in a house. It's old but it's in good condition."

"I love old houses!"

I personally didn't care anything about old houses. I was happy with the house we were living in then, one that was about the same age I was. I still don't like old houses. But that was me and that was Mother.

Her conversation with my camp peer continued to be pleasant and didn't end until we got to the clearing where the campers' parents had parked, and he joined his own parents.

I stashed my suitcase in the trunk and then got in the front passenger seat of my mother's car. Getting out of a field full of cars and people was slow and awkward. I am just glad I was not the one driving. While Mother was making her way out of this makeshift parking lot, I caught a glimpse of Stacy. She noticed me. She waved at me, and I waved back hoping Mother wouldn't notice. She made it out of the clearing onto the road. She navigated the back roads and eventually got us to the Interstate highway.

I was in a daze on the way home. I just stared ahead with a goofy smile on my face. I was silent. This was all because I was totally smitten by love. "You've been awfully quiet," Mother seemed baffled by my dazed condition. "Are you all right?"

"Everything's great," I managed to say. I am sure my mother was wondering what in the world had happened to me. When we got to Portland, we stopped at a fast food breakfast place. We went inside. As we stood in line to place our order at the counter, I thought about my desire to share my world with Stacy. I wanted to tell her about my school and the great friends I had there. I thought about what it would be like if Stacy were able to visit me and see our home. I could show her my book collection in my bedroom. We were not in line for long. Mother placed her order and tried to take my order by saying "and he'll have...." I did not respond. I was in dreamland. "Tom," she finally had to say.

"Uh, yes. I'll have …." I had to study the menu on the wall because I had not even looked at it until Mother got my attention. After an embarrassing moment, I ordered something. We took our food and sat at a table in the dining area. As we ate, I was working up the courage to tell Mother about my romantic encounter. I felt like I owed her an explanation.

"Mother, I'm sorry I have been so spaced out, but I can explain," I said. "I met a cute girl at camp."

"That's great!"

"I was in the Round Chapel minding my own business and suddenly out of nowhere, this very pretty girl asked me to sit by her."

"What's her name?"

"Stacy."

"Where is she from?"

"She lives in Lakota which is a very small town in Washington. I have her address."

"Are you going to write her?"

"Eventually."

"Well, that's just great!"

When we left the fast food place and got home, I went to my room and put my suitcase to the side. First let me tell you something about myself. Ever since I was a small child, I have loved maps. On road trips with my family, I would have a road atlas out and my finger on the place on the map wherever we were. Thus, I always had an atlas in my bedroom. The first thing I did when I got to my bedroom was look at my road atlas to find Lakota. I looked in the index in the back of the atlas where they have the list of cities and towns for each state. It would list the name of the town, its population, and, most importantly to me, its location. The location was identified by number letter coordinates. I found the listing for Lakota. Its population was listed as 845. I went back to the Washington state map in the atlas and found Lakota. I also noted the county in which Lakota was located. *Tyler.* This had already been implied to me by Stacy when she told me she was about to enter Tyler County High School. Lakota appeared to be close to 150 kilometers away.

I took the piece of paper with Stacy's address on it. As far as I was concerned this piece of paper was a piece of gold. I would cherish it and never let it go. I kissed the piece of paper and put it in one of the small drawers of my desk. It was the same desk that I used to do my homework during the school year.

Chapter Eighteen

Later in 1985 and Beyond

After that day I spent a week at home before going back to camp for another week. That second non-consecutive week of camp was not nearly as memorable. What I remember best is that I got sick that week of camp and went home on my second full day of camp.

After that second week of camp, I spent another week at home. Then my family and I went on a vacation on the coast which for a family reunion. I met my second cousins and their parents from Florida. The family reunion involved everyone descended from my great-grandfather on my maternal grandfather's side who was alive and able to attend.

When I got home from this vacation, I decided that the time was right to write a letter to Stacy. If I had written Stacy the first week after I got home from camp, any response she sent might not have gotten to my house until I went back to camp. I guess my parents could have saved it for me or even forwarded it to camp for me, but I really wanted to be home if and when I got that letter from her. If I had written the letter when I got back from my second week of camp, her response might arrive when none of us were home and were instead at the aforementioned family reunion. I think my parents would have arranged for a neighbor to get our mail for us while we were out of town, but I was not taking any chances. I could have written Stacy from camp during my second week, but I would have had to clarify that I wanted her to send any response to my home and not to camp. I also would have had to take the piece of paper with her address with me to camp and I cherished it too much to take a chance of losing it at camp. Either that or I would have had to make a copy of the address on a piece of paper of my own and taken it to camp. I guess I could have done that. Instead, I began my letter to Stacy on the day that both camp sessions and the family reunion vacation were behind me.

I reached into the drawer which had Stacy's address in it and put her address on the top of my desk. Then I opened another drawer in my desk and got out a loose-leaf piece of lined paper no different from the paper I use for school. I got a pen with an eraser and erasable ink which I usually used for school. Given the importance of this letter to me, I wanted to make sure I could erase any mistakes I made. I also made sure it was a fresh eraser because I didn't want there to be any smudges which tends to happen with these erasable pens when the eraser has had a lot of use. I recalled reading *Peanuts* comic strip books in which Charlie Brown was unable to have a pen pal because he had such bad luck using pens with leaking ink and struggling to handwrite. He could only have a pencil pal, so he began his letters with "Dear Pencil Pal." I hoped that I would have better luck than Charlie Brown.

I put pen and paper to begin my letter. The first thing was to put the date on the top line in the upper right corner.

August 5, 1985

Then I began the main body of my letter.

Dear Stacy:
It was very exciting to meet you at Camp Sunbeam. Your friend, Isabella, seemed nice too.

Let me tell you about myself. I live in Portland. No. Actually, I live in a suburb of Portland.

Then I began racking my brain for what to say next about myself.

Then I decided to stick with the basics and began telling her about my family including my father's occupation and my siblings. I mentioned our cats as being family members. I told her the name of my school even though I think I remembered mentioning that when I was with her at camp. I ended the paragraph by saying this about my school:

I am very happy there and have many friends there.

The next paragraph was questions I had about her.

I would love to know more about you. What is your family like? What have you done this summer besides go to camp?

I did the courtesy of telling her about my own summer after asking about hers.

After our week at camp together, I spent a week at home. Then I had another one-week session at Camp Sunbeam. Then I was at home for another week followed by a week at the beach. This beach vacation was actually a family reunion at which I met my second cousin from Florida.

My closing paragraph went as follows:

I am glad we both had loads of fun at camp. I wish you the best of luck in the upcoming school year.

I signed the letter at the bottom with my first name in bigger handwriting than the rest of the letter with a crude dash before my name.

To my amazement, I was able to get through the letter without having to do any erasures with my Eraser Mate pen. I was glad because those erasures tend to be messy especially when the eraser is worn down.

I needed an envelope. I went to my mother who was sitting on a couch in the den.

"Mom, I need an envelope. Do we have any?" I asked.

"There should be some in my kitchen desk drawer." She had a built-in desk in the kitchen which she used as a home office.

"I am writing a letter to that girl I met at camp." I decided to go ahead and tell Mom about my intentions even though it was a little embarrassing. I wanted to head her off before she started probing.

"That's great!" was her reaction.

I went into the kitchen and checked multiple drawers until I found an envelope that was the appropriate size and shape for my letter. I returned to the desk in my bedroom and wrote Stacy's name and address on the front of the envelope. Then I wrote my name and address in the upper left corner of the envelope to serve as a return address. I was particularly careful when writing the return address. First, I did not write it in cursive but in block letters. Second, I made the return address almost as big as the mailing address. I did not want to take any chances that Stacy would not be able to read it and use the address to respond to my letter. If Stacy did not respond, I did not want it to be because of my bad handwriting. In fact, I had not yet sealed the letter in because I wanted to be able to write my address in the body of the letter if I was unable to write it clearly on the envelope.

I folded the letter appropriately and placed it in the envelope. I sealed the envelope by licking it. *Yuk.* In the privacy of my room, I kissed the line along which it was sealed while looking forward to the possibility of kissing Stacy in person. I had to go back to Mom's desk in the kitchen for the last step: placing the stamp on the letter.

I took the letter to the mailbox in front of our house, opened the door of the mailbox, placed the letter in the mailbox, closed the mailbox door, and raised the red flag of the mailbox. At that point, it was all up to the United States Postal Service.

I decided to busy myself by picking up sticks in the front lawn so Dad could mow it later. When I finished doing that, I went inside and began reading a book in my bedroom. While I was reading the book, I heard the unmistakable sound of the small mail truck driving to our mailbox and opening and closing the mailbox. I looked out the window and sure enough, I saw the familiar mail truck. The mail carrier then drove to the next house. I had goosebumps as I felt a special thrill inside me. The letter was on its way to Stacy.

I did not expect there to be a letter from Stacy when I checked our mail the next day. I had only checked it because Mom asked me to do so. When I got the mail the third day, I tingled with the excitement that seeing a letter from Stacy in the mailbox was a reasonable possibility. I felt the same tingling on the fourth day. By the fifth day, I was starting to have to tell myself "Give her time." After ten days, my anxiety had melted into disappointment. If she had responded immediately, the letter would have gotten to me by then. Maybe she was busy with other things, but it was summer and therefore it seemed less likely that she was too busy. On the eleventh day, I was having the same thoughts when I went to the mailbox. I opened its door and pulled out the contents. There was one of my parents' magazines, a bill for a payment on Dad's car, a flyer ad, two more bills, and there was an envelope shaped differently from the ones the bills came in. Also, the mailing address on the front was large and handwritten, not typewritten as was the case with the bills. The letter was addressed to me. My excitement level went way up instantly. I checked the return address. It was Stacy's name and address!

First, I jumped up in celebration by the mailbox. Then I ran to our front door jumping over the two steps leading to our small patio at the front door with my fists clenched and my feet landing safely on the patio. I went inside the house and handed the rest of the mail to my mother who was sitting on the couch in the den saying, "Here's the mail, Mom." I would wait until I had actually read the letter from Stacy before telling her the great news. Here's why. It is only great news if the possibility of a relationship is still intact after reading the letter. It was possible that Stacy was saying in the letter that I was a creep, and she didn't want to hear (or get a letter) from me again. Maybe she would more gently send that message by saying that she felt it was best that we stop corresponding. Even if the letter was friendly, if I saw the simple two-word phrase "my boyfriend" anywhere in the letter, my heart would break instantly.

I tore the letter open in a way and got the treasure out of the envelope. I had a prickling feeling in my fingers as I unfolded it. She had written on lined paper just as I had in my letter to her.

Then I went back to the privacy of my bedroom to open and read the letter.

Dear Tom:

Thank you so much for your letter. It had a great time at camp. I was great to meet you. You're sweet.

I think I mentioned this when we were at camp, but my mom works in the cafeteria at our elementary school and my dad works at the bank. I know I told you about my sister. We also have a golden retriever.

I am looking forward to school too. I am going to do color guard in the school band. Color guard is those girls who twirl the flags in the band.

Have a great school year.

Stacy

I put both the letter and the envelope separately on my desk. Then I went to the den to explain to my mother why I retreated to my room so quickly after handing her the mail. "I got a letter from that girl I met at camp."

"That's wonderful, Tom."

Later that afternoon, I rode my bicycle to a friend's house to tell him the happy news. I started from the beginning when Stacy asked me to sit by her. I eventually got to the letter. Perhaps the best thing about good things happening to you are sharing the experience with friends and family.

The next day, I wrote another letter to Stacy. I described my celebration when I got a letter back from her. This time, I included my phone number and told her she was welcome to call me. I had to include the area code since it would be a long-distance call. A few days later, Stacy responded with a letter to me. The message contained the usual pleasantries and a funny story about her family's dog. What I noticed was that it did not include her phone number. Okay. Maybe she wants to just be pen pals. I did write another letter to her. However, I waited several weeks to do so. I wanted to wait until well after school started so I would have some school adventures to tell her about. I continued my life at school in academics and extracurricular activities throughout the fall, winter, and spring break without a response from Stacy.

Shortly after spring break, I saw Adam Craig visiting my school. He was sitting with his brother who happened to be a student at my school and a good friend of mine. Adam was also dating one of the girls at my school. She was also present at that lunch table. It was great to see him, of course. Adam told me that Stacy was going to be a leader-in-training at Camp Sunbeam. He also told me that Stacy would be in Portland with her grandmother and that he would see to it that she called me. I gladly handed over my phone number.

That Saturday, while I was at home, the phone rang, and I jumped. The call, however, was not from Stacy and it was not even for me. After waiting most of the day for Stacy to call, I called Adam. He informed me that Stacy's grandmother was very sick. I could have asked for the phone number for where Stacy was, but I did not want to bother her when she was dealing with this.

I did go to Camp Sunbeam that next summer in 1986 to work as an assistant for the director, my friend Benjamin Heimer. I hoped that Stacy would be there that week that I was there, but she was not.

Ever since I experienced this incredible romance, I wanted to know more about Stacy's hometown and school. What I found out about her hometown and school several years later broke my heart.

The principal of Tyler County High School called a school-wide assembly and asked the student body if there would be any interracial couples at the prom. When at least one of the students indicated that they would have an interracial date, the principal announced that the prom was cancelled. One of the students was a biracial girl who wanted to bring her White boyfriend to the prom. This created quite a dilemma for her since it was not possible for any date of hers to be of the same race as herself. When she asked the principal what she was supposed to do, the principal reportedly told her that her parents had made a mistake when they had her. I felt incredible sadness for this girl who at that moment could only break down and tearfully say, "My God doesn't make mistakes."

A few days later this principal reinstated the prom, but the damage had already been done. It was obvious that this principal did not need to be in a position where he could shape policy that governed our children.

This controversy dragged on for months and not surprisingly got plenty of media attention. The Tyler County Board of Education considered removing this principal from office but ultimately decided to keep him. A 1960's style freedom school was set up as an alternative for those who did not want to go to Tyler County High School as long as this man was principal. The Tyler County High School prom took place as originally planned. The biracial girl who was humiliated by the principal in front of her fellow students went to this prom and to an alternative prom that had been set up. However, there was still the matter of the racist principal being in office.

The United States Justice Department got involved. No one backed down. The Ku Klux Klan held a rally in Lakota. Then one August night, Tyler County High School burned to the ground. The principal and another man were caught on camera attacking a news camera operator from a television station. I remember feeling my heart break as I watched this play out on television. Two days later, this principal was "reassigned" to the school district's central office.

I remember how badly I wished these things about Lakota were not true. If it had been any other small town, I would have dismissed it as just another example of a small town being backwards and an example of a place where I would not want to raise my children. But I associated this small town with sweet memories. Now those memories had been soiled.

I have often pondered why that one summer week had such an impact on my consciousness. Maybe because it had so many coming-of-age moments, a decision to follow Christ, first date, first time away from home and on my own (actually I should probably say "one of my first times away from home" since I had been at camp twice before in previous years). I had been very good at math and science during school and that summer my mind was already bored with such simple subjects and was working on something much harder: how to interact with girls.

In retrospect, that summer seems like a happier time in my life. I was full of hope and optimism about the future. Then again, someday when I am much older, I may look back on this year 2023 and think of this as the good old days. It is easy for me to forget that sixteen-years-old was also an age of anxiety, insecurity, and inexperience in the game of life.

At any rate, I will never forget the gauntlet of emotions I experienced that week. I will always remember the comradery of our hut. I will never forget how I felt when a pretty girl asked me to sit by her. I will always marvel at the drama of the whole week

After spending an hour cooking dinner, my attention turned to present-day affairs. I turned on the news again. "It looks like Camp Sunbeam will be spared from the wildfire," a news announcer droned on. "Firefighters now estimate that the fire is spreading to the west, not the south where the camp is located. Other structures will not be so fortunate. There is a gas station, several houses, and a restaurant which are in the imminent path of the fire."

I felt relief. It is not that I didn't feel bad for those who did or were about to lose property in that fire. It is that I would not lose a place that had sentimental value to me. It would remain possible that maybe in the future I would once again walk on the grounds where I bonded with hut-mates, received guidance from leaders and camp staff, and went on my first date. I knew I would never walk the halls of the school where Stacy began the ninth grade after experiencing a summer camp romance with me.

I finished cooking dinner just in time. Just as I put my wife's dinner plate on the dinner table, she opened the door to the house. I decided to make sure she knew where I was. "I'm in here, Arianna."